The Birds' Christmas Carol

AND

Polly Oliver's Problem

The Birds' Christmas Carol

TOGETHER WITH ITS SEQUEL

Polly Oliver's Problem

By

KATE DOUGLAS WIGGIN

A Thrushwood Book

PUBLISHERS *Grosset & Dunlap* NEW YORK

Illustrated by REISIE LONETTE

PRINTED IN THE UNITED STATES OF AMERICA

The Birds' Christmas Carol

Contents

I

A Little Snow Bird

IT WAS very early Christmas morning, and in the stillness of the dawn, with the soft snow falling on the housetops, a little child was born in the Bird household.

They had intended to name the baby Lucy, if it were a girl; but they had not expected her on Christmas morning, and a real Christmas baby was not to be lightly named—the whole family agreed in that.

They were consulting about it in the nursery. Mr. Bird said that he had assisted in naming the three boys, and that he should leave this matter entirely to Mrs.

9

Bird; Donald wanted the child called "Dorothy," after a pretty, curly-haired girl who sat next him in school; Paul chose "Luella," for Luella was the nurse who had been with him during his whole babyhood, up to the time of his first trousers, and the name suggested all sorts of comfortable things. Uncle Jack said that the first girl should always be named for her mother, no matter how hideous the name happened to be.

Grandma said that she would prefer not to take any part in the discussion, and everybody suddenly remembered that Mrs. Bird had thought of naming the baby Lucy, for Grandma herself; and, while it would be indelicate for her to favor that name, it would be against human nature for her to suggest any other, under the circumstances.

Hugh, the "hitherto baby," if that is a possible term, sat in one corner and said nothing, but felt, in some mysterious way, that his nose was out of joint; for there was a newer baby now, a possibility he had never taken into consideration; and the "first girl," too—a still higher development of treason, which made him actually green with jealousy.

But it was too profound a subject to be settled then and there, on the spot; besides, Mamma had not been asked, and everybody felt it rather absurd, after all, to forestall a decree that was certain to be absolutely wise, just, and perfect.

The reason that the subject had been brought up at all so early in the day lay in the fact that Mrs. Bird never allowed her babies to go overnight unnamed. She was a person of so great decision of character that she would have blushed at such a thing; she said that to let blessed babies go dangling and dawdling about without names, for months and months, was enough to ruin them for life. She also said that if one could not make up one's mind in twenty-four hours it was a sign that— But I will not repeat the rest, as it might prejudice you against the most charming woman in the world.

So Donald took his new bicycle and went out to ride up and down the stone pavement and notch the shins of innocent people as they passed by, while Paul spun his musical top on the front steps.

But Hugh refused to leave the scene of action. He seated himself on the top stair in the hall, banged his head against the railing a few times, just by way of uncorking the vials of his wrath, and then subsided into gloomy silence, waiting to declare war if more "first girl babies" were thrust upon a family already surfeited with that unnecessary article.

Meanwhile dear Mrs. Bird lay in her room, weak, but safe and happy, with her sweet girl baby by her side and the heaven of motherhood opening again before her. Nurse was making gruel in the kitchen, and the room was dim and quiet. There was a cheerful open fire in the grate, but though the shutters were closed, the side windows that looked out on the Church of Our Saviour, next door, were a little open.

Suddenly a sound of music poured out into the bright air and drifted into the chamber. It was the boy choir singing Christmas anthems. Higher and higher rose the clear, fresh voices, full of hope and cheer, as children's voices always are. Fuller and fuller grew the burst of melody as one glad strain fell upon another in joyful harmony:

> *"Carol, brothers, carol,*
>   *Carol joyfully,*
> *Carol the good tidings,*
>   *Carol merrily!*
> *And pray a gladsome Christmas*
>   *For all your fellow-men:*
> *Carol, brothers, carol,*
>   *Christmas Day again."*

One verse followed another, always with the same sweet refrain:

> *"And pray a gladsome Christmas*
>   *For all your fellow-men:*
> *Carol, brothers, carol,*
>   *Christmas Day again."*

Mrs. Bird thought, as the music floated in upon her gentle sleep, that she had slipped into heaven with her new baby, and that the angels were bidding them welcome. But the tiny bundle by her side stirred a little, and though it was scarcely more than the ruffling of a feather, she awoke; for the mother-ear is so close to the heart that it can hear the faintest whisper of a child.

She opened her eyes and drew the baby closer. It looked like a rose dipped in milk, she thought, this pink and white blossom of girlhood, or like a pink cherub, with its halo of pale yellow hair, finer than floss silk.

> *"Carol, brothers, carol,*
>   *Carol joyfully,*
> *Carol the good tidings,*
>   *Carol merrily!"*

The voices were brimming over with joy.

"Why, my baby," whispered Mrs. Bird in soft surprise, "I had forgotten what day it was. You are a little Christmas child, and we will name you 'Carol'—Mother's Christmas Carol!"

"What!" said Mr. Bird, coming in softly and closing the door behind him.

"Why, Donald, don't you think 'Carol' is a sweet name for a Christmas baby? It came to me just a moment ago in the singing, as I was lying here half asleep and half awake."

"I think it is a charming name, dear heart, and sounds just like you, and I hope that, being a girl, this baby has some chance of being as lovely as her mother"—at which speech from the baby's papa, Mrs. Bird, though she was as weak and tired as she could be, blushed with happiness.

And so Carol came by her name.

Of course, it was thought foolish by many people, though Uncle Jack declared laughingly that it was very strange if a whole family of Birds could not be indulged in a single Carol; and Grandma, who adored the child, thought the name much more appropriate than Lucy, but was glad that people would probably think it short for Caroline.

Perhaps because she was born in holiday time, Carol was a very happy baby. Of course, she was too tiny to understand the joy of Christmastide, but people say there is everything in a good beginning, and she may have breathed in unconsciously the fragrance of evergreens and holiday dinners; while the peals of sleigh bells and the laughter of happy children may have fallen upon her baby ears and wakened in them a glad surprise at the merry world she had come to live in.

Her cheeks and lips were as red as holly berries; her hair was for all the world the color of a Christmas candle flame; her eyes were bright as stars; her laugh like a chime of Christmas bells, and her tiny hands forever outstretched in giving.

Such a generous little creature you never saw! A spoonful of bread and milk had always to be taken by Mamma or nurse before Carol could enjoy her supper; whatever bit of cake or sweetmeat found its way into her pretty fingers was straightway broken in half to be shared with Donald, Paul, or Hugh; and when they made believe nibble the morsel with affected enjoyment, she would clap her hands and crow with delight.

"Why does she do it?" asked Donald thoughtfully. "None of us boys ever did."

"I hardly know," said Mamma, catching her darling to her heart, "except that she is a little Christmas child, and so she has a tiny share of the blessedest birthday the world ever knew!"

II

Drooping Wings

It was December, ten years later.

Carol had seen nine Christmas trees lighted on her birthdays, one after another; nine times she had assisted in the holiday festivities of the household, though in her babyhood her share of the gaieties was somewhat limited.

For five years, certainly, she had hidden presents for Mamma and Papa in their own bureau drawers, and harbored a number of secrets sufficiently large to burst a baby brain, had it not been for the relief gained by whispering them all to Mamma, at night, when she was in her crib, a proceeding which did not in the least lessen the value of a secret in her innocent mind.

For five years she had heard "'Twas the Night Before Christmas," and hung up a scarlet stocking many sizes too large for her, and pinned a sprig of holly on her little white nightgown, to show Santa Claus that she was a "truly" Christmas child, and dreamed of fur-coated saints and toy-packs and reindeer, and wished everybody a "Merry Christmas" before it was light in the morning, and lent every one of her new toys to the neighbors' children before noon, and eaten turkey and plum pudding, and gone to bed at night in a trance of happiness at the day's pleasures.

Donald was away at college now. Paul and Hugh were great manly fellows, taller than their mother. Papa Bird had gray hairs in his whiskers; and Grandma, God bless her, had been four Christmases in heaven.

But Christmas in the Birds' Nest was scarcely as merry now as it used to be in the bygone years, for the little child, that once brought such an added blessing to the day, lay month after month a patient, helpless invalid, in the room where she was born. She had never been very strong in body, and it was with a pang of terror her mother and father noticed, soon after she was five years old, that she began to limp, ever so slightly; to complain too often of weariness, and to nestle close to her mother, saying she "would rather not go out to play, please." The illness was slight at first, and hope was always stirring in Mrs. Bird's heart. "Carol would feel stronger in the summertime"; or, "She would be better when she had spent a year in the country"; or, "She would outgrow it"; or, "They would try a new physician"; but by and by it came to be all too sure that no physician save One could make Carol strong again, and that no "summertime" nor "country air," unless it were the everlasting summertime in a heavenly country, could bring back the little girl to health.

The cheeks and lips that were once as red as holly berries faded to faint pink; the starlike eyes grew softer, for they often gleamed through tears; and the gay child-laugh, that had been like a chime of Christmas bells, gave place to a smile so lovely, so touching, so tender and patient, that it filled every corner of the house with a gentle radiance that might have come from the face of the Christ Child himself.

Love could do nothing; and when we have said that we have said all, for it is stronger than anything else in the whole wide world. Mr. and Mrs. Bird were talking it over one evening, when all the children were asleep. A famous physician had visited them that day, and told them that some time, it might be in one year, it might be in more, Carol would slip quietly off into heaven, whence she came.

"It is no use to close our eyes to it any longer," said Mr. Bird, as he paced up and down the library floor, "Carol will never be well again. It almost seems as if I could not bear it when I think of that loveliest child doomed to lie there day after day, and, what is still more, to suffer pain that we are helpless to keep away from her. Merry Christmas, indeed; it gets to be the saddest day in the year to me!"—and poor Mr. Bird sank into a chair by the table, and buried his face in his hands to keep his wife from seeing the tears that would come in spite of all his efforts.

"But, Donald, dear," said sweet Mrs. Bird, with trembling voice, "Christmas Day may not be so merry with us as it used, but it is very happy, and that is better, and very blessed, and that is better yet. I suffer chiefly for Carol's sake, but I have almost given up being sorrowful for my own. I am too happy in the child, and I see too clearly what she has done for us and the other children. Donald and Paul and Hugh were three strong, willful, boisterous boys, but now you seldom see such tenderness, devotion, thought for others, and self-denial in lads of their years. A quarrel or a hot word is almost unknown in this house, and why? Carol would hear it, and it would distress her, she is so full of love and goodness. The boys study with all their might and main. Why? Partly, at least, because they like to teach Carol, and amuse her by telling her what they read. When the seamstress comes, she likes to sew in Miss Carol's room, because there she forgets her own troubles, which, Heaven knows, are sore enough! And as for me, Donald, I am a better woman every day for Carol's sake; I have to be her eyes, ears, feet, hands— her strength, her hope; and she, my own little child, is my example!"

"I was wrong, dear heart," said Mr. Bird more cheerfully; "we will try not to repine, but to rejoice instead, that we have an 'angel of the house.'"

"And as for her future," Mrs. Bird went on, "I think

we need not be overanxious. I feel as if she did not belong altogether to us, but that when she has done what God sent her for, He will take her back to Himself— and it may not be very long!" Here it was poor Mrs. Bird's turn to break down, and Mr. Bird's turn to comfort her.

III

The Birds' Nest

───────

CAROL herself knew nothing of motherly tears and fatherly anxieties; she lived on peacefully in the room where she was born.

But you never would have known that room; for Mr. Bird had a great deal of money, and though he felt sometimes as if he wanted to throw it all in the sea, since it could not buy a strong body for his little girl, yet he was glad to make the place she lived in just as beautiful as it could be.

The room had been extended by the building of a large addition that hung out over the garden below, and was so filled with windows that it might have been a conservatory. The ones on the side were thus still nearer the Church of Our Saviour than they used to be; those in front looked out on the beautiful harbor, and those in the back commanded a view of nothing in particular but a narrow alley; nevertheless, they were pleasantest of all to Carol, for the Ruggles family lived in the alley, and the nine little, middle-sized, and big Ruggles children were a source of inexhaustible interest.

The shutters could all be opened and Carol could take a real sun bath in this lovely glass house, or they could all be closed when the dear head ached or the dear eyes were tired. The carpet was of soft gray, with clusters of green bay and holly leaves. The furniture was of white wood, on which an artist had painted snow scenes and Christmas trees and groups of merry children ringing bells and singing carols.

Donald had made a pretty, polished shelf, and screwed it on the outside of the footboard, and the boys always kept this full of blooming plants, which they changed from time to time; the headboard, too, had a bracket on either side, where there were pots of maidenhair ferns.

Lovebirds and canaries hung in their golden houses in the windows, and they, poor caged things, could hop as far from their wooden perches as Carol could venture from her little white bed.

On one side of the room was a bookcase filled with hundreds—yes, I mean it—with hundreds and hundreds of books; books with gay-colored pictures, books without; books with black and white outline sketches, books with none at all; books with verses, books with

Maidenhair ferns hung from brackets on either side

stories; books that made children laugh, and some, only a few, that made them cry; books with words of one syllable for tiny boys and girls, and books with words of fearful length to puzzle wise ones.

This was Carol's "Circulating Library." Every Saturday she chose ten books, jotting their names down in a diary; into these she slipped cards that said:

> *Please keep this book two weeks and read it.*
> *With love,*
> *Carol Bird*

Then Mrs. Bird stepped into her carriage and took the ten books to the Children's Hospital, and brought home ten others that she had left there the fortnight before.

This was a source of great happiness; for some of the Hospital children that were old enough to print or write, and were strong enough to do it, wrote Carol sweet little letters about the books, and she answered them, and they grew to be friends. (It is very funny, but you do not always have to see people to love them. Just think about it, and tell me if it isn't so.)

There was a high wainscoting of wood about the room, and on top of this, in a narrow gilt framework, ran a row of illuminated pictures, illustrating fairy tales, all in dull blue and gold and scarlet and silver. From the door to the closet there was the story of "The Fair One with Golden Locks"; from closet to bookcase, ran "Puss in Boots"; from bookcase to fireplace, was "Jack the Giant-Killer"; and on the other side of the room were "Hop o' my Thumb," "The Sleeping Beauty," and "Cinderella."

Then there was a great closet full of beautiful things to wear, but they were all dressing gowns and slippers and shawls; and there were drawers full of toys and games, but they were such as you could play with on your lap. There were no ninepins, nor balls, nor bows and arrows, nor bean bags, nor tennis rackets; but, after all, other children needed these more than Carol Bird, for she was always happy and contented, whatever she had or whatever she lacked; and after the room had been made so lovely for her, on her eighth Christmas, she always called herself, in fun, a "Bird of Paradise."

On these particular December days she was happier than usual, for Uncle Jack was coming from England to spend the holidays. Dear, funny, jolly, loving, wise Uncle Jack, who came every two or three years, and brought so much joy with him that the world looked as black as a thundercloud for a week after he went away again.

The mail had brought this letter:

LONDON, *November* 28, 188–

Wish you merry Christmas, you dearest birdlings in America! Preen your feathers, and stretch the Birds' Nest a trifle, if you please, and let Uncle Jack in for the holidays. I am coming with such a trunk full of treasures that you'll have to borrow the stockings of Barnum's Giant and Giantess; I am coming to squeeze a certain little ladybird until she cries for mercy; I am coming to see if I can find a boy to take care of a black pony that I bought lately. It's the strangest thing I ever knew; I've hunted all over Europe, and can't find a boy to suit me! I'll tell you why. I've set my heart on finding one with a dimple in his chin, because this pony particularly likes dimples! ["Hurrah!" cried Hugh, "bless my dear dimple; I'll never be ashamed of it again."]

Please drop a note to the clerk of the weather, and have a good, rousing snowstorm—say on the twenty-second. None of your meek, gentle, nonsensical, shilly-shallying snowstorms; not the sort where the flakes float lazily down from the sky as if they didn't care whether they ever got here or not and then melt away as soon as they touch the earth, but a regular businesslike whizzing, whirring, blurring, cutting snowstorm, warranted to freeze and stay on!

I should like rather a LARGE Christmas tree, if it's convenient: not one of those "sprigs," five or six feet high, that you used to have three or four years ago, when the birdlings were not fairly feathered out; but a tree of some size. Set it up in the garret, if necessary, and then we can cut a hole in the roof if the tree chances to be too high for the room.

Tell Bridget to begin to fatten a turkey. Tell her that by the twentieth of December that turkey must not be able to stand on its legs for fat, and then on the next three days she must allow it to recline easily on its side, and stuff it to bursting. (One ounce of stuffing beforehand is worth a pound afterward.)

The pudding must be unusually huge, and darkly, deeply, lugubriously blue in color. It must be stuck so full of plums that the pudding itself will ooze out into the pan and not be brought on to the table at all. I expect to be there by the twentieth, to manage these little things myself—remembering it is the early Bird that catches the worm—but give you the instructions in case I should be delayed.

And Carol must decide on the size of the tree—she knows best, she was a Christmas child; and she must plead for the snowstorm—the "clerk of the weather" may pay some attention to her; and she must look up the boy with the dimple for me—she's likelier to find him than I am, this minute. She must advise about the turkey, and Bridget must bring the pudding to her bedside and let her drop every separate plum into it and stir it once for luck, or I'll not eat a single slice—for Carol is the dearest part of Christmas to Uncle Jack, and he'll have none of it without her. She is better than all the turkeys and puddings and apples and spareribs and wreaths and garlands and mistletoe and stockings and chimneys and sleigh bells in Christendom! She is the very sweetest Christmas Carol that was ever written, said, sung, or chanted, and I am coming as fast as ships and railway trains can carry me, to tell her so.

Carol's joy knew no bounds. Mr. and Mrs. Bird laughed like children and kissed each other for sheer delight, and when the boys heard it they simply whooped like wild Indians; until the Ruggles family, whose back yard joined their garden, gathered at the door and wondered what was "up" in the big house.

IV

"Birds of a Feather Flock Together"

UNCLE JACK did really come on the twentieth. He was not detained by business, nor did he get left behind nor snowed in, as frequently happens in stories, and in real life too, I am afraid. The snowstorm came also; and the turkey nearly died a natural and premature death from overeating. Donald came, too; Donald, with a line of down upon his upper lip, and Greek and Latin on his tongue, and stories of knowledge in his handsome head, and stories—bless me, you couldn't turn over a chip without reminding Donald of something that happened "at college." One or the other was always at Carol's bedside, for they fancied her paler than she used to be, and they could not bear her out of sight. It was Uncle

Jack, though, who sat beside her in the winter twi-lights. The room was quiet, and almost dark, save for the snow-light outside, and the flickering flame of the fire, that danced over the "Sleeping Beauty's" face and touched the Fair One's golden locks with ruddier glory. Carol's hand (all too thin and white these latter days) lay close clasped in Uncle Jack's, and they talked to-gether quietly of many, many things.

"I want to tell you all about my plans for Christmas this year, Uncle Jack," said Carol, on the first evening of his visit, "because it will be the loveliest one I ever had. The boys laugh at me for caring so much about it; but it isn't altogether because it is Christmas, nor be-cause it is my birthday; but long, long ago, when I first began to be ill, I used to think, the first thing when I waked on Christmas morning, 'Today is Christ's birth-day—*and mine!*' I did not put the words close together, you know, because that made it seem too bold; but I first said, 'Christ's birthday,' out loud, and then, in a minute, softly to myself—'*and mine!*' 'Christ's birthday —*and mine!*' And so I do not quite feel about Christ-mas as other girls do. Mamma says she supposes that ever so many other children have been born on that day. I often wonder where they are, Uncle Jack, and whether it is a dear thought to them, too, or whether I am so much in bed, and so often alone, that it means more to me. Oh, I do hope that none of them are poor, or cold, or hungry; and I wish—I wish they were all as happy as I, because they are really my little brothers and sisters. Now, Uncle Jack dear, I am going to try and make somebody happy every single Christmas that

I live, and this year it is to be the 'Ruggleses in the rear.' "

"That large and interesting brood of children in the little house at the end of the back garden?"

"Yes; isn't it nice to see so many together?—and,

Uncle Jack, why do the big families always live in the small houses, and the small families in the big houses? We ought to call them the Ruggles children, of course; but Donald began talking of them as the 'Ruggleses in the rear,' and Papa and Mamma took it up, and now we cannot seem to help it. The house was built for Mr. Carter's coachman, but Mr. Carter lives in Europe, and the gentleman who rents his place for him doesn't care what happens to it, and so this poor family came to live there. When they first moved in, I used to sit in my window and watch them play in their back yard; they are so strong, and jolly, and good-natured—and then, one day, I had a terrible headache, and Donald asked them if they would please not scream quite so loud, and they explained that they were having a game of circus, but that they would change and play 'Deaf and Dumb Asylum' all the afternoon."

"Ha, ha, ha!" laughed Uncle Jack, "what an obliging family, to be sure!"

"Yes, we all thought it very funny, and I smiled at them from the window when I was well enough to be up again. Now, Sarah Maud comes to her door when the children come home from school, and if Mamma nods her head, 'Yes,' that means 'Carol is very well,' and then you ought to hear the little Ruggleses yell—I believe they try to see how much noise they can make; but if Mamma shakes her head, 'No,' they always play at quiet games. Then, one day, Cary, my pet canary, flew out of her cage, and Peter Ruggles caught her and brought her back, and I had him up here in my room to thank him."

"Is Peter the oldest?"

"No; Sarah Maud is the oldest—she helps do the washing; and Peter is the next. He is a dressmaker's boy."

"And which is the pretty little red-haired girl?"

"That's Kitty."

"And the fat youngster?"

"Baby Larry."

"And that—most freckled one?"

"Now, don't laugh—that's Peoria."

"Carol, you are joking."

"No, really, Uncle dear. She was born in Peoria, that's all."

"And is the next boy Oshkosh?"

"No," laughed Carol, "the others are Susan, and Clement, and Eily, and Cornelius; they all look exactly alike, except that some of them have more freckles than the others."

"How did you ever learn all their names?"

"Why, I have what I call a 'window-school.' It is too cold now; but in warm weather I am wheeled out on my balcony, and the Ruggleses climb up and walk along our garden fence, and sit down on the roof of our carriage house. That brings them quite near, and I tell them stories. On Thanksgiving Day they came up for a few minutes—it was quite warm at eleven o'clock —and we told each other what we had to be thankful for; but they gave such queer answers that Papa had to run away for fear of laughing; and I couldn't understand them very well. Susan was thankful for 'trunks,' of all things in the world; Cornelius, for 'horsecars'; Kitty, for 'pork steak'; while Clem, who is very quiet, brightened up when I came to him, and said he was thankful for his 'lame puppy.' Wasn't that pretty?"

"It might teach some of us a lesson, mightn't it, little girl?"

"That's what Mamma said. Now I'm going to give this whole Christmas to the Ruggleses; and, Uncle Jack, I earned part of the money myself."

"You, my bird? How?"

"Well, you see, it could not be my own, own Christmas if Papa gave me all the money, and I thought to really keep Christ's birthday I ought to do something of my very own; and so I talked with Mamma. Of course she thought of something lovely; she always does: Mamma's head is just brimming over with lovely thoughts—all I have to do is ask, and out pops the very one I want. This thought was to let her write down, just as I told her, a description of how a child lived in her own room for three years, and what she did to amuse herself; and we sent it to a magazine and got twenty-five dollars for it. Just think!"

"Well, well," cried Uncle Jack, "my little girl a real author! And what are you going to do with this wonderful 'own' money of yours?"

"I shall give the nine Ruggleses a grand Christmas dinner here in this very room—that will be Papa's contribution—and afterward a beautiful Christmas tree, fairly blooming with presents—that will be my part; for I have another way of adding to my twenty-five dollars, so that I can buy nearly anything I choose. I should like it very much if you would sit at the head of the table, Uncle Jack, for nobody could ever be frightened of you, you dearest, dearest, dearest thing that ever was! Mamma is going to help us, but Papa and the boys are going to eat together downstairs for fear of making the little Ruggleses shy; and after we've had a merry time with the tree we can open my window and all listen together to the music at the evening church service, if it comes before the children go. I have written a letter to the organist, and asked him if I might have the two songs I like best. Will you see if it is all right?"

BIRDS' NEST, *December* 21, 188–

DEAR MR. WILKIE—I am the little girl who lives next door to the church, and, as I seldom go out, the music on practice days and Sundays is one of my greatest pleasures.

I want to know if you can have "Carol, Brothers, Carol," on Christmas night, and if the boy who sings "My Ain Countree" so beautifully may please sing that too. I think it is the loveliest thing in the world, but it always makes me cry; doesn't it you?

If it isn't too much trouble, I hope they can sing them both quite early, as after ten o'clock I may be asleep.

Yours respectfully,

CAROL BIRD

P.S.—The reason I like "Carol, Brothers, Carol," is because the choirboys sang it ten years ago, the morning I was born, and put it into Mamma's head to call me Carol. She didn't remember then that my other name would be Bird, because she was half asleep, and could only think of one thing at a time. Donald says if I had been born on the Fourth of July they would have named me "Independence," or if on the twenty-second of February, "Georgina," or even "Cherry," like Cherry in "Martin Chuzzlewit"; but I like my own name and birthday best.

Yours truly,

CAROL BIRD

Uncle Jack thought the letter quite right, and did not even smile at her telling the organist so many family items.

The days flew by as they always fly in holiday time, and it was Christmas Eve before anybody knew it. The family festival was quiet and very pleasant, but almost overshadowed by the grander preparations for the next day. Carol and Elfrida, her pretty German nurse, had ransacked books, and introduced so many plans, and plays, and customs, and merrymakings from Germany, and Holland, and England, and a dozen other countries, that you would scarcely have known how or where you were keeping Christmas. Even the dog and the cat had enjoyed their celebration under Carol's direction. Each had a tiny table with a lighted candle in the center, and a bit of Bologna sausage placed very near it; and everybody laughed till the tears stood in their eyes to see Villikins and Dinah struggle to nibble the sausages, and at the same time to evade the candle flame. Villikins barked, and sniffed, and howled in impatience, and after many vain attempts succeeded in dragging off the prize, though he singed his nose in doing it. Dinah, meanwhile, watched him placidly, her delicate nostrils quivering with expectation, and, after all excitement had subsided, walked with dignity to the table, her beautiful gray satin tail sweeping behind her, and, calmly putting up one velvet paw, drew the sausage gently down, and walked out of the room without turning a hair, so to speak. Elfrida had scattered handfuls of seed over the snow in the garden, that the wild birds might have a comfortable breakfast next morning, and had stuffed bundles of dry grasses in the fireplaces, so that the reindeer of Santa Claus could refresh themselves after their long gallops across country. This was really only done for fun, but it pleased Carol.

And when, after dinner, the whole family had gone to the church to see the Christmas decorations, Carol limped out on her slender crutches, and with Elfrida's help, placed all the family boots in a row in the upper hall. That was to keep the dear ones from quarreling all through the year. There were Papa's stout top boots; Mamma's pretty buttoned shoes next; then Uncle Jack's, Donald's, Paul's, and Hugh's; and at the end of the line her own little white worsted slippers. Last, and sweetest of all, like the children in Austria, she put a lighted candle in her window to guide the dear Christ Child, lest He should stumble in the dark night as He passed up the deserted street. This done, she dropped into bed, a rather tired, but very happy Christmas fairy.

V

Some Other Birds Are Taught to Fly

BEFORE the earliest Ruggles could wake and toot his five-cent tin horn, Mrs. Ruggles was up and stirring about the house, for it was a gala day in the family. Gala day! I should think so! Were not her nine "childern" invited to a dinner party at the great house, and weren't they going to sit down free and equal with the mightiest in the land? She had been preparing for this grand occasion ever since the receipt of Carol Bird's invitation, which, by the way, had been speedily enshrined in an old photograph frame and hung under the looking glass in the most prominent place in the kitchen, where it stared the occasional visitor directly in the eye, and made him livid with envy:

BIRDS' NEST, *December* 17, 188–

DEAR MRS. RUGGLES—I am going to have a dinner party on Christmas Day, and would like to have all your children come. I want them every one, please, from Sarah Maud to Baby Larry. Mamma says dinner will be at half past five, and the Christmas tree at seven; so you may expect them home at nine o'clock. Wishing you a Merry Christmas and a Happy New Year, I am

Yours truly,

CAROL BIRD

Breakfast was on the table promptly at seven o'clock, and there was very little of it, too; for it was an excellent day for short rations, though Mrs. Ruggles heaved a sigh as she reflected that the boys, with their India-rubber stomachs, would be just as hungry the day after the dinner party as if they had never had any at all.

As soon as the scanty meal was over, she announced the plan of the campaign: "Now, Susan, you an' Kitty wash up the dishes; an' Peter, can't yer spread up the beds, so't I can git ter cuttin' out Larry's new suit? I ain't satisfied with his clo'es, an' I thought in the night of a way to make him a dress out o' my old red plaid shawl—kind o' Scotch style, yer know, with the fringe 't the bottom.—Eily, you go find the comb an' take the snarls out the fringe, that's a lady! You little young ones clear out from underfoot! Clem, you an' Con hop into bed with Larry while I wash yer underflannins; 'twon't take long to dry 'em.—Yes, I know it's bothersome, but yer can't go int' s'ciety 'thout takin' some trouble, 'n' anyhow I couldn't git round to 'em last night.—Sarah Maud, I think 'twould be perfeckly han'som' if you ripped them brass buttons off yer uncle's *po*liceman's coat 'n' sewed 'em in a row up the front o' yer green skirt. Susan, you must iron out yours 'n' Kitty's apurns; 'n' there, I come mighty near forgettin' Peory's stockin's! I counted the whole lot last night when I was washin' of 'em, 'n' there ain't but nineteen anyhow yer fix 'em, 'n' no nine pairs mates nohow; 'n' I ain't goin' ter have my childern wear odd stockin's to a dinner comp'ny, fetched up as I was!—Eily, can't you run out an' ask Mis' Cullen ter lend me a pair o' stockin's for Peory, 'n' tell her if she will, Peory'll give Jim half her candy when she gets home. Won't yer, Peory?"

Peoria was young and greedy, and thought the remedy so out of all proportion to the disease that she set up a deafening howl at the projected bargain—a howl so rebellious and so entirely out of season that her mother started in her direction with flashing eye and uplifted hand; but she let it fall suddenly, saying, "No, I vow I won't lick ye Christmas Day, if yer drive me crazy; but speak up smart, now, 'n' say whether yer'd ruther give Jim Cullen half yer candy or go barelegged ter the party?" The matter being put so plainly, Peoria collected her faculties, dried her tears, and chose the lesser evil, Clem having hastened the decision by an affectionate wink that meant he'd go halves with her on his candy.

"That's a lady!" cried her mother. "Now, you young ones that ain't doin' nothin', play all yer want ter be-

fore noontime, for after ye git through eatin' at twelve
o'clock me 'n' Sarah Maud's goin' ter give yer sech a
washin' 'n' combin' 'n' dressin' as yer never had before
'n' never will ag'in likely, 'n' then I'm goin' to set yer
down 'n' give yer two solid hours trainin' in manners;
'n' 'twon't be no foolin' neither."

"All we've got ter do's go eat!" grumbled Peter.

"Well, that's enough," responded his mother; "there's
more'n one way of eatin', let me tell yer, 'n' you've got
a heap ter learn about it, Peter Ruggles. Land sakes, I
wish you children could see the way I was fetched up
to eat. I never took a meal o' vittles in the kitchen before I married Ruggles; but yer can't keep up that style
with nine young ones 'n' yer pa always off ter sea."

The big Ruggleses worked so well, and the little
Ruggleses kept from "underfoot" so successfully, that
by one o'clock nine complete toilets were laid out in
solemn grandeur on the beds. I say, "complete," but I
do not know whether they would be called so in the
best society. The law of compensation had been well
applied: he that had necktie had no cuffs; she that had
sash had no handkerchief, and *vice versa,* but they all
had shoes and a certain amount of clothing, such as it
was, the outside layer being in every case quite above
criticism.

"Now, Sarah Maud," said Mrs. Ruggles, her face
shining with excitement, "everything's red up an' we
can begin. I've got a boiler 'n' a kettle 'n' a pot o' hot
water. Peter, you go into the back bedroom, 'n' I'll take
Susan, Kitty, Peory, 'n' Cornelius; 'n' Sarah Maud, you

take Clem, 'n' Eily, 'n' Larry, one to a time. Scrub 'em 'n' rinse 'em, or, 'tany rate, git fur's yer can with 'em, 'n' then I'll finish 'em off while you do yerself."

Sarah Maud couldn't have scrubbed with any more decision and force if she had been doing floors, and the little Ruggleses bore it bravely, not from natural heroism, but for the joy that was set before them. Not being satisfied, however, with the "tone" of their complexions, and feeling that the number of freckles to the square inch was too many to be tolerated in the highest social circles, she wound up operations by applying a little Bristol brick from the knife-board, which served as the proverbial "last straw," from under which the little Ruggleses issued rather red and raw and out of temper. When the clock struck four they were all clothed, and most of them in their right minds, ready for those last touches that always take the most time.

Kitty's red hair was curled in thirty-four ringlets, Sarah Maud's was braided in one pigtail, and Susan's and Eily's in two braids apiece, while Peoria's resisted all advances in the shape of hair oils and stuck out straight on all sides, like that of the Circassian girl of the circus—so Clem said; and he was sent into the bedroom for it, too, from whence he was dragged out forgivingly, by Peoria herself, five minutes later. Then, exciting moment, came linen collars for some and neckties and bows for others—a magnificent green glass breastpin was sewed into Peter's purple necktie—and Eureka! the Ruggleses were dressed, and Solomon in all his glory was not arrayed like one of these!

A row of seats was then formed directly through the

middle of the kitchen. Of course, there were not quite chairs enough for ten, since the family had rarely wanted to sit down all at once, somebody always being out or in bed, or otherwise engaged, but the wood box and the coal hod finished out the line nicely, and nobody thought of grumbling. The children took their places according to age, Sarah Maud at the head and Larry on the coal hod, and Mrs. Ruggles seated herself in front, surveying them proudly as she wiped the sweat of honest toil from her brow.

"Well," she exclaimed, "if I do say so as shouldn't, I never see a cleaner, more stylish mess o' childern in my life! I do wish Ruggles could look at ye for a minute!— Larry Ruggles, how many times have I got ter tell yer not ter keep pullin' at yer sash? Haven't I told yer if it comes ontied, yer waist 'n' skirt'll part comp'ny in the middle, 'n' then where'll yer be?—Now, look me in the eye, all of yer! I've of'en told yer what kind of a family the McGrills was. I've got reason to be proud, goodness knows! Your uncle is on the *po*lice force o' New York City; you can take up the paper most any day an' see his name printed right out—James McGrill—'n' I can't have my childern fetched up common, like some folks'; when they go out they've got to have clo'es, and learn to act decent! Now, I want ter see how yer goin' to behave when yer git there tonight. 'Tain't so awful easy as you think 'tis. Let's start in at the beginnin' 'n' act out the whole business. Pile into the bedroom, there, every last one o' ye, 'n' show me how yer goin' to go int' the parlor. This'll be the parlor, 'n' I'll be Mis' Bird."

The youngsters hustled into the next room in high glee, and Mrs. Ruggles drew herself up in the chair with an infinitely haughty and purse-proud expression that much better suited a descendant of the McGrills than modest Mrs. Bird.

The bedroom was small, and there presently ensued such a clatter that you would have thought a herd of wild cattle had broken loose. The door opened, and they straggled in, all the younger ones giggling, with Sarah Maud at the head, looking as if she had been caught in the act of stealing sheep; while Larry, being last in line, seemed to think the door a sort of gate of heaven which would be shut in his face if he didn't get there in time; accordingly he struggled ahead of his elders and disgraced himself by tumbling in head fore-most.

Mrs. Ruggles looked severe. "There, I knew yer'd do it in some sech fool way! Now, go in there an' try it over ag'in, every last one o' ye, 'n' if Larry can't come in on two legs he can stay ter home—d'yer hear?"

The matter began to assume a graver aspect; the little Ruggleses stopped giggling and backed into the bedroom, issuing presently with lock step, Indian file, a scared and hunted expression on every countenance.

"No, no, no!" cried Mrs. Ruggles, in despair. "That's worse yet; yer look for all the world like a gang o' pris'ners! There ain't no style ter that: spread out more, can't yer, 'n' act kind o' careless-like—nobody's goin' ter kill ye! That ain't what a dinner party is!"

The third time brought deserved success, and the

pupils took their seats in the row. "Now, yer know," said Mrs. Ruggles impressively, "there ain't enough decent hats to go round, 'n' if there was I don' know's I'd let yer wear 'em, for the boys would never think to take 'em off when they got inside, for they never do—but, anyhow, there ain't enough good ones. Now, look me in the eye. You're only goin' jest round the corner; you needn't wear no hats, none of yer, 'n' when yer get int' the parlor, 'n' they ask yer ter lay off yer hats, Sarah Maud must speak up 'n' say it was sech a pleasant evenin' 'n' sech a short walk that yer left yer hats to home. Now, can yer remember?"

All the little Ruggleses shouted, "Yes, marm!"

"What have *you* got ter do with it?" demanded their mother. "Did I tell *you* to say it? Warn't I talkin' ter Sarah Maud?"

The little Ruggleses hung their diminished heads. "Yes, marm," they piped, more discreetly.

"Now, we won't leave nothin' to chance; git up, all of ye, an' try it.—Speak up, Sarah Maud."

Sarah Maud's tongue clove to the roof of her mouth. "Quick!"

"Ma thought—it was—sech a pleasant hat that we'd —we'd better leave our short walk to home," recited Sarah Maud, in an agony of mental effort.

This was too much for the boys. An earthquake of suppressed giggles swept all along the line.

"Oh, whatever shall I do with yer?" moaned the unhappy mother. "I s'pose I've got to learn it to yer!" —which she did, word for word, until Sarah Maud

thought she could stand on her head and say it back-
ward.

"Now, Cornelius, what are *you* goin' ter say ter make
yerself good comp'ny?"

"Do? Me? Dunno!" said Cornelius, turning pale with
unexpected responsibility.

"Well, ye ain't goin' to set there like a bump on a
log 'thout sayin' a word ter pay for yer vittles, air ye?

Ask Mis' Bird how she's feelin' this evenin', or if Mr.
Bird's hevin' a busy season, or how this kind o' weather
agrees with him, or somethin' like that.—Now, we'll
make b'lieve we've got ter the dinner—that won't be
so hard, 'cause yer'll have somethin' to do—it's awful
bothersome to stan' round an' act stylish.—If they have
napkins, Sarah Maud down to Peory may put 'em in
their laps, 'n' the rest of ye can tuck 'em in yer necks.
Don't eat with yer fingers—don't grab no vittles off
one 'nother's plates; don't reach out for nothin', but

wait till yer asked, 'n' if you never *git* asked don't git up an' grab it.—Don't spill nothin' on the tablecloth, or like's not Mis' Bird'll send yer away from the table—'n' I hope she will if yer do! (Susan! keep your handkerchief in your lap where Peory can borry it if she needs it, 'n' I hope she'll know when she does need it, though I don't expect it.) Now, we'll try a few things ter see how they'll go! Mr. Clement, do you eat cramb'ry sarse?"

"Bet yer life!" cried Clem, who in the excitement of the moment had not taken in the idea exactly and had mistaken this for an ordinary bosom-of-the-family question.

"Clement McGrill Ruggles, do you mean to tell me that you'd say that to a dinner party? I'll give ye one more chance. Mr. Clement, will you take some of the cramb'ry?"

"Yes, marm, thank ye kindly, if you happen ter have any handy."

"Very good indeed! But they won't give yer two tries tonight—yer just remember that!—Miss Peory, do you speak for white or dark meat?"

"I ain't perticler as ter color—anything that nobody else wants will suit me," answered Peory with her best air.

"First rate! Nobody could speak more genteel than that. Miss Kitty, will you have hard or soft sarse with your pudden?"

"Hard or soft? Oh! A little of both, if you please, an' I'm much obliged," said Kitty, bowing with decided ease and grace; at which all the other Ruggleses pointed the finger of shame at her, and Peter *grunted* expressively, that their meaning might not be mistaken.

"You just stop your gruntin', Peter Ruggles; that warn't greedy, that was all right. I wish I could git it inter your heads that it ain't so much what yer say, as the way you say it. An' don't keep starin' cross-eyed at your necktie pin, or I'll take it out 'n' sew it on to Clem or Cornelius: Sarah Maud'll keep her eye on it, 'n' if it turns broken side out she'll tell yer. Gracious! I shouldn't think you'd ever seen nor worn no jool'ry in your life.—Eily, you an' Larry's too little to train, so you just look at the rest an' do's they do, 'n' the Lord have mercy on ye 'n' help ye to act decent! Now, is there anything more ye'd like to practice?"

"If yer tell me one more thing, I can't set up an' eat," said Peter gloomily. "I'm so cram full o' manners now, I'm ready ter bust, 'thout no dinner at all."

"Me, too," chimed in Cornelius.

"Well, I'm sorry for yer both," rejoined Mrs. Ruggles sarcastically. "If the 'mount o' manners yer've got on hand now troubles ye, you're dreadful easy hurt! Now, Sarah Maud, after dinner, about once in so often, you must git up 'n' say, 'I guess we'd better be goin',' 'n' if they say, 'Oh, no, set a while longer,' yer can set; but if they don't say nothin', you've got ter get up 'n' go. —Now, hev yer got that int' yer head?"

"About once in so often!" Could any words in the language be fraught with more terrible and wearing uncertainty?

"Well," answered Sarah Maud mournfully, "seems as if this whole dinner party set right square on top o' me! Mebbe I could manage my own manners, but to manage nine mannerses is worse'n staying to home!"

"Oh, don't fret," said her mother, good-naturedly, now that the lesson was over, "I guess you'll git along. I wouldn't mind if folks would only say, 'Oh, childern will be childern'; but they won't. They'll say, 'Land o' Goodness, who fetched them childern up?'—It's quarter past five, 'n' yer can go now:—remember 'bout the hats—don't all talk ter once—Susan, lend yer han'k'-chief ter Peory—Peter, don't keep screwin' yer scarf pin —Cornelius, hold yer head up straight—Sarah Maud, don't take yer eyes off o' Larry, 'n', Larry, you keep holt o' Sarah Maud 'n' do jest as she says—'n' whatever you do, all of yer, never forgit for one second that yer mother was a McGrill."

VI

"When the Pie Was Opened"

THE CHILDREN went out of the back door quietly, and were presently lost to sight, Sarah Maud slipping and stumbling along absent-mindedly, as she recited rapidly under her breath, "Itwassuchapleasantevenin'n'sucha shortwalk . . . thatwethoughtwe'dleaveourhatstohome. —Itwassuchapleasantevenin'n'suchashortwalk . . . that wethoughtwe'dleaveourhatstohome."

Peter rang the doorbell, and presently a servant admitted them, and, whispering something in Sarah's ear, drew her downstairs into the kitchen. The other Ruggleses stood in horror-stricken groups as the door closed behind their commanding officer; but there was no time for reflection, for a voice from above was heard, saying, "Come right upstairs, please!"

"*Theirs not to make reply,*
Theirs not to reason why,
Theirs but to do or die."

Accordingly they walked upstairs, and Elfrida, the nurse, ushered them into a room more splendid than anything they had ever seen. But, oh, woe! where was Sarah Maud! and was it Fate that Mrs. Bird should say, at once, "Did you lay your hats in the hall?" Peter felt himself elected by circumstance the head of the family, and, casting one imploring look at tongue-tied Susan, standing next him, said huskily, "It was so very pleasant —that—that—" "That we hadn't good hats enough to go 'round," put in little Susan bravely, to help him out, and then froze with horror that the ill-fated words had slipped off her tongue.

However, Mrs. Bird said pleasantly, "Of course you wouldn't wear hats such a short distance—I forgot when I asked. Now, will you come right in to Miss Carol's room? She is so anxious to see you."

Just then Sarah Maud came up the back stairs, so radiant with joy from her secret interview with the cook that Peter could have pinched her with a clear conscience; and Carol gave them a joyful welcome. "But where is Baby Larry?" she cried, looking over the group with searching eye. "Didn't he come?"

"Larry! Larry!" Good gracious, where was Larry? They were all sure that he had come in with them, for Susan remembered scolding him for tripping over the doormat. Uncle Jack went into convulsions of laughter. "Are you sure there were nine of you?" he asked.

"I think so, sir," said Peoria timidly, "but anyhow,

there was Larry." And she showed signs of weeping.

"Oh, well, cheer up!" cried Uncle Jack. "Probably he's not lost—only mislaid. I'll go and find him before you can say Jack Robinson!"

"I'll go, too, if you please, sir," said Sarah Maud, "for it was my place to mind him, an' if he's lost I can't relish my vittles!"

The other Ruggleses stood rooted to the floor. Was this a dinner party, forsooth; and if so, why were such things ever spoken of as festive occasions?

Sarah Maud went out through the hall, calling, "Larry! Larry!" and without any interval of suspense a thin voice piped up from below, "Here I be!"

The truth was that Larry, being deserted by his natural guardian, dropped behind the rest, and wriggled into the hat tree to wait for her, having no notion of walking unprotected into the jaws of a fashionable entertainment. Finding that she did not come, he tried to crawl from his refuge and call somebody, when— dark and dreadful ending to a tragic day—he found that he was too much intertwined with umbrellas and canes to move a single step. He was afraid to yell (when I have said this of Larry Ruggles I have pictured a state of helpless terror that ought to wring tears from every eye); and the sound of Sarah Maud's beloved voice, some seconds later, was like a strain of angel music in his ears. Uncle Jack dried his tears, carried him upstairs, and soon had him in breathless fits of laughter, while Carol so made the other Ruggleses forget themselves that they were presently talking like accomplished diners-out.

Sarah Maud's voice was like music in his ears

Carol's bed had been moved into the farthest corner of the room, and she was lying on the outside, dressed in a wonderful dressing gown that looked like a fleecy cloud. Her golden hair fell in fluffy curls over her white forehead and neck, her cheeks flushed delicately, her eyes beamed with joy, and the children told their mother, afterwards, that she looked as beautiful as the angels in the picture books.

There was a great bustle behind a huge screen in another part of the room, and at half past five this was taken away, and the Christmas dinner table stood revealed. What a wonderful sight it was to the poor little Ruggles children, who ate their sometimes scanty meals on the kitchen table! It blazed with tall colored candles, it gleamed with glass and silver, it blushed with flowers, it groaned with good things to eat; so it was not strange that the Ruggleses, forgetting altogether that their mother was a McGrill, shrieked in admiration of the fairy spectacle. But Larry's behavior was the most disgraceful, for he stood not upon the order of his going, but went at once for a high chair that pointed unmistakably to him, climbed up like a squirrel, gave a comprehensive look at the turkey, clapped his hands in ecstasy, rested his fat arms on the table, and cried with joy, "I beat the hull lot o' yer!" Carol laughed until she cried, giving orders, meanwhile —"Uncle Jack, please sit at the head, Sarah Maud at the foot, and that will leave four on each side; Mamma is going to help Elfrida, so that the children need not look after each other, but just have a good time."

A sprig of holly lay by each plate, and nothing would do but each little Ruggles must leave his seat and have it pinned on by Carol, and as each course was served, one of them pleaded to take something to her. There was hurrying to and fro, I can assure you, for it is quite a difficult matter to serve a Christmas dinner on the third floor of a great city house; but if it had been necessary to carry every dish up a rope ladder the servants would gladly have done so. There were turkey and chicken, with delicious gravy and stuffing, and there were half a dozen vegetables, with cranberry jelly, and celery, and pickles; and as for the way these delicacies were served, the Ruggleses never forgot it as long as they lived.

Peter nudged Kitty, who sat next him, and said, "Look, will yer, ev'ry feller's got his own partic'lar butter; I s'pose that's to show you can eat that 'n' no more. No, it ain't either, for that pig of a Peory's just gettin' another helpin'!"

"Yes," whispered Kitty, "an' the napkins is marked with big red letters! I wonder if that's so nobody'll nip 'em; an' oh, Peter, look at the pictures stickin' right on ter the dishes! Did yer ever?"

"The plums is all took out o' my cramb'ry sarse an' it's friz to a stiff jell'!" whispered Peoria, in wild excitement.

"Hi—yah! I got a wishbone!" sang Larry, regardless of Sarah Maud's frown; after which she asked to have his seat changed, giving as excuse that he "gen'ally set beside her, an' would feel strange"; the true reason being that she desired to kick him gently, under the table, whenever he passed what might be termed "the McGrill line."

"I declare to goodness," murmured Susan, on the other side, "there's so much to look at I can't scarcely eat nothin'!"

"Bet yer life I can!" said Peter, who had kept one servant busily employed ever since he sat down; for, luckily, no one was asked by Uncle Jack whether he would have a second helping, but the dishes were quietly passed under their noses, and not a single Ruggles refused anything that was offered him, even unto the seventh time.

Then, when Carol and Uncle Jack perceived that more turkey was a physical impossibility, the meats were taken off and the dessert was brought in—a dessert that would have frightened a strong man after such a dinner as had preceded it. Not so the Ruggleses—for a strong man is nothing to a small boy—and they kindled to the dessert as if the turkey had been a dream and the six vegetables an optical delusion. There were plum pudding, mince pie, and ice cream; and there were nuts, and raisins, and oranges. Kitty chose ice cream, explaining that she knew it "by sight, though she hadn't never tasted none"; but all the rest took the entire variety, without any regard to consequences.

"My dear child," whispered Uncle Jack, as he took Carol an orange, "there is no doubt about the necessity of this feast, but I do advise you after this to have them twice a year, or quarterly perhaps, for the way these children eat is positively dangerous; I assure you I tremble for that terrible Peoria."

"Never mind," laughed Carol, "let them have enough for once; it does my heart good to see them, and they shall come oftener next year."

The feast being over, the Ruggleses lay back in their chairs languidly, like little gorged boa constrictors, and the table was cleared in a trice. Then a door was opened into the next room, and there, in a corner facing Carol's bed, which had been wheeled as close as possible, stood the brilliantly lighted Christmas tree, glittering with gilded walnuts and tiny silver balloons, and wreathed with snowy chains of popcorn. The presents had been bought mostly with Carol's story money, and were selected after long consultations with Mrs. Bird. Each girl had a blue knitted hood, and each boy a red crocheted comforter, all made by Mamma, Carol, and Elfrida. ("Because if you buy everything, it doesn't show so much love," said Carol.) Then every girl had a pretty plaid dress of a different color, and every boy a warm coat of the right size. Here the useful presents stopped, and they were quite enough; but Carol had pleaded to give them something "for fun." "I know they need the clothes," she had said, when they were talking over the matter just after Thanksgiving, "but they don't care much for them, after all. Now, Papa, won't you *please* let me go without part of my presents this year, and give me the money they would cost, to buy something to amuse the Ruggleses?"

"You can have both," said Mr. Bird promptly. "Is there any need of my little girl's going without her own Christmas, I should like to know? Spend all the money you like."

"But that isn't the thing," objected Carol, nestling close to her father; "it wouldn't be mine. What is the use? Haven't I almost everything already, and am I not the happiest girl in the world this year, with Uncle Jack and Donald at home? You know very well it is more blessed to give than to receive; so why won't you let me do it? You never look half as happy when you are getting your presents as when you are giving us ours. Now, Papa, submit, or I shall have to be very firm and disagreeable with you!"

"Very well, your Highness, I surrender."

"That's a dear Papa! Now what were you going to give me? Confess!"

"A bronze figure of Santa Claus; and in the 'little round belly that shakes when he laughs like a bowlful of jelly,' is a wonderful clock—oh, you would never give it up if you could see it!"

"Nonsense." laughed Carol. "As I never have to get up to breakfast, nor go to bed, nor catch trains, I think my old clock will do very well! Now, Mamma, what were you going to give me?"

"Oh, I hadn't decided. A few more books, and a gold thimble, and a smelling-bottle, and a music box, perhaps."

"Poor Carol," laughed the child merrily, "she can afford to give up these lovely things, for there will still be left Uncle Jack, and Donald, and Paul, and Hugh, and Uncle Rob, and Aunt Elsie, and a dozen other people to fill her Christmas stocking!"

So Carol had her way, as she generally did; but it was usually a good way, which was fortunate, under

the circumstances; and Sarah Maud had a set of Miss
Alcott's books, and Peter a modest silver watch, Cornelius a tool chest, Clement a doghouse for his lame
puppy, Larry a magnificent Noah's ark, and each of
the younger girls a beautiful doll.

You can well believe that everybody was very merry
and very thankful. All the family, from Mr. Bird down
to the cook, said that they had never seen so much
happiness in the space of three hours; but it had to end,
as all things do. The candles flickered and went out, the
tree was left alone with its gilded ornaments, and Mrs.
Bird sent the children downstairs at half past eight,
thinking that Carol looked tired.

"Now, my darling, you have done quite enough for
one day," said Mrs. Bird, getting Carol into her little
nightgown. "I'm afraid you will feel worse tomorrow,
and that would be a sad ending to such a charming
evening."

"Oh, wasn't it a lovely, lovely time," sighed Carol. "From first to last, everything was just right. I shall never forget Larry's face when he looked at the turkey; nor Peter's when he saw his watch; nor that sweet, sweet Kitty's smile when she kissed her dolly; nor the tears in poor, dull Sarah Maud's eyes when she thanked me for her books; nor—"

"But we musn't talk any longer about it tonight," said Mrs. Bird anxiously, "you are too tired, dear."

"I am not so very tired, Mamma. I have felt well all day; not a bit of pain anywhere. Perhaps this has done me good."

"Perhaps; I hope so. There was no noise or confusion; it was just a merry time. Now, may I close the door and leave you alone, dear? Papa and I will steal in softly by and by to see if you are all right; but I think you need to be very quiet."

"Oh, I'm willing to stay by myself; but I am not sleepy yet, and I am going to hear the music, you know."

"Yes, I have opened the window a little, and put the screen in front of it, so that you won't feel the air."

"Can I have the shutters open? And won't you turn my bed, please? This morning I woke ever so early, and one bright, beautiful star shone in that eastern window. I never noticed it before, and I thought of the Star in the East, that guided the wise men to the place where the baby Jesus was. Good night, Mamma. Such a happy, happy day!"

"Good night, my precious Christmas Carol—Mother's blessed Christmas child."

"Bend your head a minute, Mother dear," whispered Carol, calling her mother back. "Mamma, dear, I do think that we have kept Christ's birthday this time just as He would like it. Don't you?"

"I am sure of it," said Mrs. Bird softly.

VII

The Birdling Flies Away

THE RUGGLESES had finished a last romp in the library with Paul and Hugh, and Uncle Jack had taken them home and stayed awhile to chat with Mrs. Ruggles, who opened the door for them, her face all aglow with excitement and delight. When Kitty and Clem showed her the oranges and nuts that they had kept for her, she astonished them by saying that at six o'clock Mrs. Bird had sent her in the finest dinner she had ever seen in her life; and not only that, but a piece of dress goods that must have cost a dollar a yard if it cost a cent.

As Uncle Jack went down the rickety steps he looked back into the window for a last glimpse of the family, as the children gathered about their mother, showing their beautiful presents again and again—and then upward to a window in the great house yonder. "A little child shall lead them," he thought. "Well, if—if anything ever happens to Carol, I will take the Ruggleses under my wing."

"Softly, Uncle Jack," whispered the boys, as he walked into the library awhile later. "We are listening to the music in the church. The choir has sung 'Carol, Brothers, Carol,' and now we think the organist is beginning to play 'My Ain Countree' for Carol."

"I hope she hears it," said Mrs. Bird, "but they are very late tonight, and I dare not speak to her lest she should be asleep. It is almost ten o'clock."

The boy soprano, clad in white surplice, stood in the organ loft. The light shone full upon his crown of fair hair, and his pale face, with its serious blue eyes, looked paler than usual. Perhaps it was something in the tender thrill of the voice, or in the sweet words, but there were tears in many eyes, both in the church and in the great house next door.

> *"I am far frae my hame,*
> *I am weary aften whiles*
> *For the langed-for hame-bringin',*
> *An' my Faether's welcome smiles;*
> *An' I'll ne'er be fu' content,*
> *Until my e'en do see*
> *The gowden gates o' heaven*
> *In my ain countree.*
>
> *"The earth is decked wi' flow'rs,*
> *Mony tinted, fresh an' gay,*
> *An' the birdies warble blythely,*
> *For my Faether made them sae;*

But these sights an' these soun's
Will as naething be to me,
When I hear the angels singin'
In my ain countree.

"Like a bairn to its mither,
A wee birdie to its nest,
I fain would be gangin' noo
Unto my Faether's breast;
For he gathers in His arms
Helpless, worthless lambs like me,
An' carries them Himsel'
To his ain countree."

There were tears in many eyes, but not in Carol's. The loving heart had quietly ceased to beat, and the "wee birdie" in the great house had flown to its "home nest." Carol had fallen asleep! But as to the song, I think perhaps, I cannot say, she heard it after all!

So sad an ending to a happy day! Perhaps—to those who were left; and yet Carol's mother, even in the freshness of her grief, was glad that her darling had slipped away on the loveliest day of her life, out of its glad content, into everlasting peace.

She was glad that she had gone as she had come, on the wings of song, when all the world was brimming over with joy; glad of every grateful smile, of every joyous burst of laughter, of every loving thought and word and deed the dear last day had brought.

Sadness reigned, it is true, in the little house behind the garden; and one day poor Sarah Maud, with a courage born of despair, threw on her hood and shawl, walked straight to a certain house a mile away, up the marble steps into good Dr. Bartol's office, falling at his feet as she cried, "Oh, sir, it was me an' our children that went to Miss Carol's last dinner party, an' if we made her worse we can't never be happy again!" Then the kind old gentleman took her rough hand in his and told her to dry her tears, for neither she nor any of her flock had hastened Carol's flight; indeed, he said that had it not been for the strong hopes and wishes that filled her tired heart, she could not have stayed long enough to keep that last merry Christmas with her dear ones.

And so the old years, fraught with memories, die, one after another, and the new years, bright with hopes, are born to take their places; but Carol lives again in every chime of Christmas bells that peal glad tidings, and in every Christmas anthem sung by childish voices.

Polly Oliver's Problem

Contents

I

A Declaration of Independence

"I have determined only one thing definitely," said
Polly Oliver, "and that is, the boarders must go. Oh,
how charming that sounds! I've been thinking it ever
since I was old enough to think, but I never cast it in
such an attractive, decisive form before. 'The Boarders
Must Go!' If I weren't obliged to set the boarders'
table, I'd work the motto on a banner this very minute,
and march up and down the plaza with it, followed by a
crowd of small boys with toy drums."

"You can't turn people out of the house on a moment's warning," said Mrs. Oliver suggestively, from the sofa.

"Certainly not. Give them twenty-four hours, if necessary. We can choose among several methods of getting rid of them. I can put up a placard with

BOARDERS, HO!

printed on it in large letters, and then assemble them in the banquet hall and make them a speech."

"You would insult them," objected Mrs. Oliver feebly, "and they are perfectly innocent."

"Insult them? Oh, mamma, how unworthy of you! I shall speak to them firmly but very gently. 'Ladies and gentlemen,' I shall begin, 'you have done your best to make palatable the class of human beings to which you belong, but you have utterly failed, and you must go! Board, if you must, ladies and gentlemen, but not here! Sap, if you must, the foundations of somebody else's private paradise, but not ours. In the words of the Poe-et, "Take thy beaks from off our door."' Then it will be over, and they will go out."

"Slink out, I should say," murmured Polly's mother.

"Very well, slink out," replied Polly cheerfully. "I should like to see them slink, after they've been rearing their crested heads round our table for generations; but I think you credit them with a sensitiveness they do not, and in the nature of things cannot, possess. There is something in the unnatural life which hardens both the boarder and those who board her. However, I don't insist on that method. Let us try bloodless eviction— set them quietly out in the street with their trunks; or strategy—put one of them in bed and hang out the smallpox flag. Oh, I can get rid of them in a week, if I once set my mind on it."

"There is no doubt of that," said Mrs. Oliver meekly.

Polly's brain continued to teem with sinister ideas.

"I shall make Mr. Talbot's bed so that the clothes will come off at the foot every night. He will remonstrate. I shall tell him that he kicks them off, and intimate that his conscience troubles him, or he would never be so restless. He will glare. I shall promise to do better, yet the clothes will come off worse and worse, and at last, perfectly disheartened, he will go. I shall tell Mr. Greenwood at the breakfast table, what I have been longing for months to tell him, that we can hear him snore, distinctly, through the partition. He will go. I shall put cold milk in Mrs. Caldwell's coffee every morning. I shall mean well, you know, but I shall forget. She will know that I mean well, and that it is only girlish absent-mindedness, but she will not endure it very long; she will go. And so, by the exercise of a little ingenuity, they will depart one by one, remarking that Mrs. Oliver's boarding house is not what it used to be; that Pauline is growing a little 'slack.'"

"Polly!" and Mrs. Oliver half rose from the sofa, "I will not allow you to call this a boarding house in that tone of voice."

"A boarding house, as I take it," argued Polly, "is a house where the detestable human vipers known as boarders are 'taken in and done for.'"

"But we have always prided ourselves on having it exactly like a family," said her mother plaintively. "You know we have not omitted a single refinement of the daintiest home life, no matter at what cost of labor and thought."

"Certainly, that's the point—and there you are, a sofa-invalid, and here am I with my disposition ruined for life; such a wreck in temper that I could blow up the boarders with dynamite and sleep peacefully after it."

"Now be reasonable, little daughter. Think how kind and grateful the boarders have been (at least almost always), how appreciative of everything we have done for them."

"Of course; it isn't every day they can secure an—an —elderly Juno like you to carve meat for them, or a— well, just for the sake of completing the figure of speech —a blooming Hebe like me (I've always wondered why it wasn't *She*be!) to dispense their tea and coffee; to say nothing of broma for Mr. Talbot, cocoa for Mr. Greenwood, cambric tea for Mrs. Hastings, and hot water for the Darlings. I have to keep a schedule, and refer to it three times a day. This alone shows that boarders aren't my vocation."

A bit of conversation gives the clue to character so easily that Mrs. Oliver and her daughter need little more description. You can see the pretty, fragile mother resting among her pillows, and I need only tell you that her dress is always black, her smile patient, her eyes full of peace, and her hands never idle save in this one daily resting-hour prescribed by the determined Miss Polly, who mounts guard during the appointed time like a jailer who expects his prisoner to escape if he removes his eagle eye for an instant.

The aforesaid impetuous Miss Polly has also told you something of herself in this brief interview. She is evidently a person who feels matters rather strongly, and who is wont to state them in the strongest terms she knows. Every word she utters shows you that, young as she looks, she is the real head of the family, and that her vigorous independence of thought and speech must be the result of more care and responsibility than ordinarily fall to the lot of a girl of sixteen.

Certain of her remarks must be taken with a grain of salt. Her assertion of willingness to blow up innocent boarders in their beds would seem, for instance, to indicate a vixenish and vindictive sort of temper quite unwarranted by the circumstances; but a glance at the girl herself contradicts the thought.

Item: A firm chin. She will take her own way if she can possibly get it; but *item:* a sweet, lovable mouth framed in dimples; a mouth that breaks into smiles at the slightest provocation, no matter how dreary the outlook; a mouth that quivers at the first tender word, and so the best of all correctives to the determined little chin below.

Item: A distinctly saucy nose; an aggressive, impertinent, spirited little nose, with a few freckles on it; a nose that probably leads its possessor into trouble occasionally.

Item: Two bright eyes, a trifle overproud and willful, perhaps, but candid and full of laughter.

Item: A head of brilliant, auburn hair; lively, independent, frisky hair, each glittering thread standing out by itself and asserting its own individuality; tempestuous hair that never "stays put"; capricious hair that escapes hairpins and comes down unexpectedly; hoydenish hair that makes the meekest hats look daring.

For the rest, a firm, round figure, no angles, everything, including elbows, in curves; blooming cheeks and smooth-skinned, taper-fingered hands tanned a very honest brown—the hands of a person who loves beauty.

Polly Oliver's love of beautiful things was a passion, and one that had little gratification. But luckily, though good music, pictures, china, furniture, and "purple and fine linen" were all conspicuous by their absence, she could feast without money and without price on the changeful loveliness of the Santa Ynez mountains, the sapphire tints of the placid Pacific, and the gorgeous splendor of the Californian wild flowers, so that her sense of beauty never starved.

Her hand was visible in the modest sitting room where she now sat with her mother; for it was pretty and homelike, although its simple decorations and furnishings had been brought together little by little during a period of two years; so that the first installments were all worn out, Polly was wont to remark plaintively, before the last additions made their appearance.

The straw matting had Japanese figures on it, while a number of rugs covered the worn places, and gave it an opulent look. The table covers, curtains, and portières were of blue jean worked in outline embroidery, and Mrs. Oliver's couch had as many pillows as that of an Oriental princess; for Polly's summers were spent camping in a canyon, and she embroidered sofa cushions and draperies with frenzy during these weeks of out-of-door life.

Upon the cottage piano was a blue Canton ginger jar filled with branches of feathery bamboo that spread its lace-like foliage far and wide over the ceiling and walls, quite covering the large spot where the roof had leaked. Various stalks of tropical-looking palms, distributed artistically about, concealed the gaping wounds in the walls, inflicted by the Benton children, who had once occupied this same apartment. Mexican water jars, bearing peacock feathers, screened Mr. Benton's two favorite places for scratching matches. The lounge was the sort of lounge that looks well only between two windows, but Polly was obliged to place it across the corner where she really needed the table, because in that position it shielded from the public view the enormous black spots on the wall where Reginald Benton had flung the ink bottle at his angel sister Pansy Belle.

Then there was an umbrella lamp bestowed by a boarder whom Mrs. Oliver had nursed through typhoid fever; a banjo; plenty of books and magazines; and an open fireplace, with a great pitcher of yellow wild flowers standing between the old-fashioned brass andirons.

Little Miss Oliver's attitude on the question of the boarders must stand quite without justification.

"It is a part of Polly," sighed her mother, "and must be borne with Christian fortitude."

Colonel Oliver had never fully recovered from a wound received in the last battle of the Civil War, and when he was laid to rest in a quiet New England churchyard, so much of Mrs. Oliver's heart was buried with him that it was difficult to take up the burden of life with any sort of courage. At last her delicate health prompted her to take the baby daughter, born after her husband's death, and go to southern California, where she invested her small property in a house in Santa Barbara. She could not add to her income by any occupation that kept her away from the baby; so the boarders followed as a matter of course (a house being suitable neither for food nor clothing), and a constantly changing family of pleasant people helped her to make both ends meet, and to educate the little daughter as she grew from babyhood into childhood.

Now, as Polly had grown up among the boarders, most of whom petted her, no one can account for her slightly ungrateful reception of their good will; but it is certain that the first time she was old enough to be trusted at the table, she grew very red in the face, slipped down from her high chair, and took her bowl of bread and milk on to the porch. She was followed and gently reasoned with, but her only explanation was that she didn't "yike to eat wiv so many peoples." Persuasion bore no fruit, and for a long time Miss Polly ate in solitary grandeur. Indeed, the feeling increased rather than diminished, until the child grew old enough to realize her mother's burden, when with passionate and protecting love she put her strong young shoulders under the load and lifted her share, never so very prettily or gracefully—it is no use trying to paint a halo round Polly's head—but with a proud courage and a sort of desperate resolve to be as good as she could, which was not very good, she would have told you.

She would come back from the beautiful home of her friend, Bell Winship, and look about on her own surroundings, never with scorn, or sense of bitterness —she was too sensible and sweet-natured for that—but with an inward rebellion against the existing state of things, and a secret determination to create a better one, if God would only give her power and opportunity. But this pent-up feeling only showed itself to her mother in bursts of impulsive nonsense, at which Mrs. Oliver first laughed and then sighed.

"Oh, for a little, little breakfast table!" Polly would say, as she flung herself on her mother's couch, and punched the pillows desperately. "Oh, for a father to say 'Steak, Polly dear?' instead of my asking, 'Steakor-chop?' over and over every morning! Oh, for a lovely, grown-up, black-haired sister, who would have hundreds of lovers, and let me stay in the room when they called! Oh, for a tiny baby brother, fat and dimpled, who would crow, and spill milk on the tablecloth, and let me sit on the floor and pick up the things he threw down! But instead of that, a new, big, strange family, different people every six months, people who don't like each other, and have to be seated at opposite ends of the table; ladies whose lips tremble with disappointment if they don't get the second joint of the chicken, and gentlemen who are sulky if anyone else gets the liver. Oh, mamma, I am sixteen now, and it will soon be

time for me to begin taking care of you; but I warn
you, I shall never do it by means of the boarders!"

"Are you so weak and proud, little daughter, as to be
ashamed because I have taken care of you these sixteen
years 'by means of the boarders,' as you say?"

"No, no, mamma! Don't think so badly of me as that.
That feeling was outgrown long ago. Do I not know
that it is just as fine and honorable as anything else in
the world, and do I not love and honor you with all my
heart because you do it in so sweet and dignified a way
that everybody respects you for it? But it isn't my vocation. I would like to do something different, something
wider, something lovelier, if I knew how, and were
ever good enough!"

"It is easy to 'dream noble things,' dear, but hard to
do them all day long. My own feeling is, if one reaches
the results one is struggling for, and does one's work as
well as it lies in one to do it, that keeping boarders is as
good service as any other bit of the world's work. One
is not always permitted to choose the beautiful or
glorious task. Sometimes all one can do is to make the
humble action fine by doing it 'as it is done in heaven.'
Remember, 'they also serve who only stand and wait.' "

"Yes, mamma," said Polly meekly, "but," stretching
out her young arms hopefully and longingly, "it must
be that they also serve who stand and *dare*, and I'm going to try that first—then I'll wait, if God wants me to."

"What if God wants you to wait first, little daughter?"

Polly hid her face in the sofa cushions and did not
answer.

II

Forecasting the Future

————

Two of Mrs. Oliver's sitting-room windows looked out
on the fig trees, and the third on a cosy veranda corner
framed in passion vines, where at the present moment
stood a round table holding a crystal bowl of Gold of
Ophir roses, a brown leather portfolio, and a dish of
apricots. Against the table leaned an old Spanish guitar
with a yellow ribbon round its neck, and across the
corner hung a gorgeous hammock of Persian colored
threads, with two or three pillows of canary-colored
China silk in one end. A bamboo lounging chair and a
Shaker rocker completed the picture; and the passer-by
could generally see Miss Anita Ferguson reclining in
the one, and a young (but not Wise) man from the
East in the other. It was not always the same young

"That's another of my troubles," said Polly

man any more than the decorations were always of the same color.

"That's another of my troubles," said Polly to her friend Margery Noble, pulling up the window shade one afternoon and pointing to the now empty "cosy corner." "I don't mind Miss Ferguson's sitting there, though it used always to be screened off for my doll-house, and I love it dearly; but she pays to sit there, and she ought to do it; besides, she looks prettier there than anyone else. Isn't it lovely? The other day she had pink oleanders in the bowl, the cushions turned the pink side up—you see they are canary and rose color— a pink muslin dress, and the guitar trimmed with a fringe of narrow pink ribbons. She was a dream, Margery! But she doesn't sit there with her young men when I am at school, nor when I am helping Ah Foy in the dining room, nor, of course, when we are at table. She sits there from four to six in the afternoon and in the evening, the only times I have with mamma in this room. We are obliged to keep the window closed, lest we should overhear the conversation. That is tiresome enough in warm weather. You see the other windows are shaded by the fig trees, so here we sit, in Egyptian darkness, mamma and I, during most of the pleasant afternoons. And if anything ever came of it, we wouldn't mind, but nothing ever does. There have been so many young men—I couldn't begin to count them, but they have worn out the seats of four chairs—and why doesn't one of them take her away? Then we could have a nice, plain young lady who would sit quietly on the front steps with the old people, and who wouldn't want me to carry messages for her three times a day."

At the present moment, however, Miss Anita Fergu-son, clad in a black habit, with a white rose in her but-tonhole, and a neat black derby with a scarf of white *crepe de Chine* wound about it, had gone on the mesa for a horseback ride, so Polly and Margery had bor-rowed the cosy corner for a chat.

Margery was crocheting a baby's afghan, and Polly was almost obscured by a rumpled yellow dress which lay in her lap.

"You observe my favorite yellow gown?" she asked.

"Yes, what have you done to it?"

"Gin Sing picked blackberries in the colander. I, sup-posing the said colander to be a pan with the usual bottom, took it in my lap and held it for an hour while I sorted the berries. Result: a hideous stain a foot and a half in diameter, to say nothing of the circumference. Mr. Greenwood suggested oxalic acid. I applied it, and removed both the stain and the dress in the follow-ing complete manner"; and Polly put her brilliant head through an immense circular hole in the front breadth of the skirt.

"It's hopeless, isn't it? for of course a patch won't look well," said Margery.

"Hopeless? Not a bit. You see this pretty yellow and white striped lawn? I have made a long, narrow apron of it, and ruffled it all round. I pin it to my waist thus, and the hole is covered. But it looks like an apron, and how do I contrive to throw the public off the scent? I add a yoke and sash of the striped lawn, and people see simply a combination-dress. I do the designing, and my beloved little mother there will do the sewing; forgetting her precious Polly's carelessness in making the hole, and remembering only her cleverness in covering it."

"Capital!" said Margery; "it will be prettier than ever. Oh dear! that dress was new when we had our last lovely summer in the canyon. Shall we ever go again, all together, I wonder? Just think how we are all scattered—the Winships traveling in Europe (I'll read you Bell's last letter by and by); Geoffrey Strong studying at Leipsic; Jack Howard at Harvard, with Elsie and her mother watching over him in Cambridge; Philip and I on the ranch as usual, and you here. We are so divided that it doesn't seem possible that we can ever have a complete reunion, does it?"

"No," said Polly, looking dreamily at the humming-birds hovering over the honeysuckle; "and if we should, everything would be different. Bless dear old Bell's heart! What a lovely summer she must be having! I wonder what she will do."

"Do?" echoed Margery.

"Yes; it always seemed to me that Bell Winship would do something in the world; that she would never go along placidly like other girls, she has so many talents."

"Yes; but so long as they have plenty of money, Dr. and Mrs. Winship would probably never encourage her in doing anything."

"It would be all the better if she could do something because she loved it, and with no thought of earning a living by it. Isn't it odd that I who most need the talents should have fewer than anyone of our dear little group? Bell can write, sing, dance, or do anything else, in fact;

Elsie can play like an angel; you can draw; but it seems to me I can do nothing well enough to earn money by it; and that is precisely what I must do."

"You've never had any special instruction, Polly dear, else you could sing as well as Bell, or play as well as Elsie."

"Well, I must soon decide. Mamma says next summer, when I am seventeen, she will try to spend a year in San Francisco and let me study regularly for some profession. The question is, what?—or whether to do something without study. I read in a magazine the other day that there are now three hundred or three thousand, I can't remember which, vocations open to women. If it were even three hundred I could certainly choose one to my liking, and there would be two hundred and ninety-nine left over for the other girls. Mrs. Weeks is trying to raise silkworms. That would be rather nice, because the worms would be silent partners in the business and do most of the work."

"But you want something without any risks, you know," said Margery sagely. "You would have to buy ground for the silkworms, and set out the mulberries, and then a swarm of horrid insects might happen along and devour the plants before the worms began spinning."

"'Competition is the life of trade,'" said Polly. "No, that isn't what I mean—'Nothing venture, nothing have,' that's it. Then how would hens do? Ever so many women raise hens."

"Hens have diseases, and they never lay very well when you have to sell the eggs. By the way, Clarence

Jones, who sings in the choir—you know, the man with the pink cheeks and cornsilk hair—advertises in the *Daily Press* for a 'live partner.' Now, there's a chance on an established hen ranch, if he doesn't demand capital or experience."

"It's a better chance for Miss Ferguson. But she doesn't like Mr. Jones, because when he comes to call, his coat pockets are always bulging with brown paper packages of a hen food that he has just invented. The other day, when he came to see her, she was out, and he handed me his card. It had a picture and advertisement of 'The Royal Dish-faced Berkshire Pig' on it; and I'm sure, by her expression when she saw it, that she will never be his 'live partner.' No, I don't think I'll have an out-of-door occupation, it's so trying to the complexion. Now, how about millinery? I could be an apprentice, and gradually rise until I imported everything direct from Paris."

"But, Polly," objected Margery, "you know you never could tie a bow, or even put a ribbon on your sailor hat."

"But I could learn. Do you suppose all the milliners were called to their work by a consciousness of genius? Perish the thought! If that were true, there wouldn't be so many hideous hats in the shop windows. However, I don't pine for millinery; it's always a struggle for me to wear a hat myself."

"You've done beautifully the last year or two, dear, and you've reaped the reward of virtue, for you've scarcely a freckle left."

"Oh, that isn't hats," rejoined Polly, "that's the law

of compensation. When I was younger, and didn't take the boarders so much to heart, I had freckles given to me for a cross; but the moment I grew old enough to see the boarders in their true light and note their effect on mamma, the freckles disappeared. Now, here's an idea. I might make a complexion lotion for a living. Let me see what I've been advised by elderly ladies to use in past years: ammonia, lemon juice, cucumbers, morning dew, milk, pork rinds, kerosene, and a few other household remedies. Of course I'm not sure which did the work, but why couldn't I mix them all in equal parts—if they would mix, you know, and let those stay out that wouldn't—and call it the 'Olivera Complexion Lotion'? The trade-mark might be a cucumber, a lemon, and a morning dewdrop, *rampant,* and a frightened little brown spot *couchant.* Then on the neat label pasted on the bottles above the trade-mark there might be a picture of a spotted girl—that's Miss Oliver before using her lotion—and a copy of my last photograph— that's Miss Oliver radiant in beauty after using her lotion."

Margery laughed, as she generally did at Polly's nonsense.

"That sounds very attractive, but if you are anxious for an elegant and dignified occupation which shall restore your mother to her ancestral position, it certainly has its defects."

"I know everything has its defects, everything except one, and I won't believe that has a single weak point."

"Oh, Polly, you deceiver! You have a secret leaning toward some particular thing, after all!"

"Yes; though I haven't talked it over fully yet, even with mamma, lest she should think it one of my wild schemes; but, Margery, I want with all my heart to be a kindergartner like Miss Mary Denison. There would be no sting to me in earning my living, if only I could do it by working among poor, ragged little children, as she does. I run in and stay half an hour with her whenever I can, and help the babies with their sewing or weaving, and I always study and work better myself afterward—I don't know whether it's the children, or Miss Denison, or the place, or all three. And the other day, when I was excused from my examinations, I stayed the whole morning in the kindergarten. When it was time for the games, and they were all in the circle, they began with a quiet play they call 'Silent Greeting,' and oh, Margery, they chose me to come in, of their own accord! When I walked into the circle to greet that smallest Walker baby my heart beat like a trip hammer, I was so afraid I should do something wrong, and they would never ask me in again. Then we played 'The Hen and Chickens,' and afterward something about the birds in the greenwood; and one of the make-believe birds flew to me (I was a tree, you know, a whispering elm tree), and built its nest in my branches, and then I smoothed its feathers and sang to it as the others had done, and it was like heaven! After the play was over, we modeled clay birds; and just as we were making the tables tidy, Professor Hohlweg came in and asked Miss Denison to come into the large hall to play for the marching, as the music teacher was absent. Then what did Miss Denison do but turn to me and say, 'Miss

Oliver, you get on so nicely with the children, would you mind telling them some little story for me? I shall be gone only ten or fifteen minutes.' Oh, Margery, it was awful! I was more frightened than when I was asked to come into the circle; but the children clapped their hands and cried, 'Yes, yes, tell us a story!' I could only think of 'The Hen That Hatched Ducks,' but I sat down and began, and, as I talked, I took my clay bird and molded it into a hen, so that they would look at me whether they listened or not. Of course, one of the big seven-year-old boys began to whisper and be restless, but I handed him a large lump of clay and asked him to make a nest and some eggs for my hen, and that soon absorbed his attention. They listened so nicely— you can hardly believe how nicely they listened! When I finished I looked at the clock. It had been nine minutes, and I couldn't think what to do the other dreadful minutes till Miss Denison should come back. At last my eye fell on the blackboard, and that gave me an idea. I drew a hen's beak and then a duck's, a hen's foot and then a duck's, to show them the difference. Just then Miss Denison came in softly, and I confess I was bursting with pride and delight. There was the blackboard with the sketches, not very good ones, it is true, the clay hen and nest and eggs, and all the children sitting quietly in their wee red chairs. And Miss Denison said, 'How charming of you to carry out the idea of the morning so nicely! My dear little girl, you were made for this sort of thing, did you know it?' "

"Well, I shouldn't think you had patience enough for any sort of teaching," said Margery candidly.

"Neither did I suppose so myself, and I haven't any patience to spare, that is, for boarders, or dishes, or beds; but I love children so dearly that they never try my patience as other things do."

"You have had the play side of the kindergarten, Polly, while Miss Denison had the care. There must be a work-a-day side to it; I'm sure Miss Denison very often looks tired to death."

"Of course!" cried Polly. "I know it's hard work; but who cares whether a thing is hard or not, if one loves it? I don't mind work; I only mind working at something I dislike and can never learn to like. Why, Margery, at the Sunday-school picnics you go off in the broiling sun and sit on a camp-chair and sketch, while I play 'Fox and Geese' with the children, and each of us pities the other and thinks she must be dying with heat. It's just the difference between us! You carry your easel and stool and paint boxes and umbrella up the steepest hill, and never mind if your back aches; I bend over Miss Denison's children with their drawing or building, and never think of my backache, do you see?"

"Yes; but I always keep up my spirits by thinking that though I may be tired and discouraged, it is worth while because it is Art I am working at; and for the sake of being an artist I ought to be willing to endure anything. You wouldn't have that feeling to inspire and help you."

"I should like to know why I wouldn't," exclaimed Polly, with flashing eyes. "I should like to know why teaching may not be an art. I confess I don't know exactly what an artist is, or rather what the dictionary definition of art is; but sit down in Miss Burke's room at the college; you can't stay there half an hour without thinking that, rather than have her teach you anything, you would be an ignorant little cannibal on a desert island! She doesn't know how, and there is nothing beautiful about it. But look at Miss Denison! When she comes into her kindergarten it is like the sunrise, and she makes everything blossom that she touches. It is all so simple and sweet that it seems as if anybody could do it; but when you try it you find that it is quite different. Whether she plays or sings, or talks or works with the children, it is perfect. 'It all seems so easy when you do it,' I said to her yesterday, and she pointed to the quotation for the day in her calendar. It was a sentence from George MacDonald: 'Ease is the lovely result of forgotten toil.' Now it may be that Miss Mary Denison is only an angel; but I *think* that she's an artist."

"On second thoughts, perhaps you are right in your meaning of the word, though it doesn't follow that all teachers are artists."

"No; nor that all the painters are," retorted Polly. "Think of that poor Miss Thomas in your outdoor class. Last week, when you were sketching the cow in front of the old barn, I sat behind her for half an hour. Her barn grew softer and softer and her cow harder and harder, till when she finished, the barn looked as if it were molded in jelly and the cow as if it were carved in red sandstone."

"She ought not to be allowed to paint," said Margery decisively.

"Of course she oughtn't! That's just what I say; and I ought not to be allowed to keep boarders, and I won't!"

"I must say you have wonderful courage, Polly. It seems so natural and easy for you to strike out for yourself in a new line that it must be you feel a sense of power, and that you will be successful."

Polly's manner changed abruptly as she glanced in at her mother's empty chair before she replied.

"Courage! Sometimes I think I haven't a morsel. I am a gilded sham. My knees tremble whenever I think of my future 'career,' as I call it. Mamma thinks me filled with a burning desire for a wider sphere of action, and so I am, but chiefly for her sake. Courage! There's nothing like having a blessed, tired little mother to take care of—a mother whom you want to snatch from the jaws of a horrible fate. That's a trifle strong, but it's dramatic! You see, Margery, a woman like my mother is not going to remain forever in her present rank in her profession—she is too superior; she is bound to rise. Now, what would become of her if she rose? Why, first, she would keep a country hotel, and sit on the front veranda in a red rocker, and chat with the commercial travelers; and then she would become the head of a summer resort, with a billiard room and a bowling alley. I must be self-supporting, and 'I will never desert Mr. Micawber,' so I should make beds and dust in Hotel Number One, and in Hotel Number Two entertain the guests with my music and my 'sprightly manners'—that's what Mr. Greenwood calls them, and the only reason I am sorry we live in a republic is that

I can't have him guillotined for doing it, but must swallow my wrath because he pays twenty dollars a week and seldom dines at home. Finally, in Hotel Number Three I should probably marry the ninepin man or the head clerk, so as to consolidate the management and save salaries, and there would end the annals of the Olivers! No, Margery!" cried Polly, waving the scissors in the air, "everybody is down on the beach, and I can make the welkin ring if I like, so hear me: The boarders must go! How, when, and where they shall go are three problems I haven't yet solved; and what I shall find to take the place of them when they do go is a fourth problem, and the knottiest one of all!"

III

The Doctor's Prescription

As THE summer wore away, Mrs. Oliver daily grew more and more languid, until at length she was forced to ask a widowed neighbor, Mrs. Chadwick, to come and take the housekeeping cares until she should feel stronger. But beef tea and drives, salt-water bathing and tonics, seemed to do no good, and at length there came a day when she had not sufficient strength to sit up.

The sight of her mother actually in bed in the day-time gave Polly a sensation as of a cold hand clutching at her heart, and she ran for Dr. Edgerton in an agony of fear. But good "Dr. George" (as he was always called, because he began practice when his father, the old doctor, was still living) came home with her, cheered her by his hopeful view of the case, and asked her to call at his office that afternoon for some remedies.

After dinner was over, Polly kissed her sleeping mother, laid a rose on her pillow for good-by, and stole out of the room.

Her heart was heavy as she walked into the office where the doctor sat alone at his desk.

"Good-day, my dear!" he said cordially, as he looked up, for she was one of his prime favorites. "Bless my soul, how you do grow, child! Why you are almost a woman!"

"I am quite a woman," said Polly, with a choking sensation in her throat, "and you have something to say to me, Dr. George, or you wouldn't have asked me to leave mamma and come here this stifling day; you would have sent the medicine by your office boy."

Dr. George laid down his pen in mild amazement. "You *are* a woman, in every sense of the word, my dear! Bless my soul, how you do hit it occasionally, you sprig of a girl! Now, sit by that window, and we'll talk. What I wanted to say to you is this, Polly. Your mother must have an entire change. Six months ago I tried to send her to a rest cure, but she refused to go anywhere without you, saying that you were her best tonic."

Two tears ran down Polly's cheeks.

"Tell me that again, please," she said softly, looking out of the window.

"She said—if you will have the very words, and all of them—that you were sun and stimulant, fresh air, medicine, and nourishment, and that she could not exist without those indispensables, even in a rest cure."

Polly's head went down on the windowsill in a sudden passion of tears.

"Hoity-toity! that's a queer way of receiving a compliment, young woman!"

She tried to smile through her April shower.

"It makes me so happy, yet so unhappy, Dr. George. Mamma has been working her strength away so many years, and I've been too young to realize it, and too young to prevent it, and now that I am grown up I am afraid it is too late."

"Not too late, at all," said Dr. George cheerily, "only we must begin at once and attend to the matter thoroughly. Your mother has been in this southern climate too long, for one thing; she needs a change of air and scene. San Francisco will do, though it's not what I should choose. She must be taken entirely away from her care, and from everything that will remind her of it; and she must live quietly, where she will not have to make a continual effort to smile and talk to people three times a day. Being agreeable, polite, and good-tempered for fifteen years, without a single lapse, will send anybody into a decline. You'll never go that way, my Polly! Now, pardon me, but how much ready money have you laid away?"

"Three hundred and twelve dollars."

"Whew!"

"It is a good deal," said Polly with modest pride; "and it would have been more yet if we had not just painted the house."

"'A good deal!' My poor lambkin! I hoped it was $1012, at least; but, however, you have the house, and that is as good as money. The house must be rented at once, furniture, boarders, and all, as it stands. It ought to bring $85 or $95 a month, in these times, and you can manage on that, with the $312 as a reserve."

"What if the tenant should give up the house as soon as we are fairly settled in San Francisco?" asked Polly, with an absolutely new gleam of caution and business in her eye.

"Brava! Why do I attempt to advise such a capable little person? Well, in the first place, there are such things as leases; and in the second place, if your tenant should move out, the agent must find you another in short order, and you will live, meanwhile, on the reserve fund. But, joking aside, there is very little risk. It is going to be a great winter for Santa Barbara, and your house is attractive, convenient, and excellently located. If we can get your affairs into such shape that your mother will not be anxious, I hope, and think, that the entire change and rest, together with the bracing air, will work wonders. I shall give you a letter to a physician, a friend of mine, and fortunately I shall come up once a month during the winter to see an old patient who insists on retaining me just from force of habit."

"And in another year, Dr. George, I shall be ready to take care of mamma myself; and then—

> "She shall sit on a cushion, and sew a fine seam,
> And feast upon strawberries, sugar, and cream."

"Assuredly, my Polly, assuredly." The doctor was pacing up and down the office now, hands in pockets, eyes on floor. "The world is your oyster; open it, my dear—open it. By the way," with a sharp turn, "with what do you propose to open it?"

"I don't know yet, but not with boarders, Dr. George."

"Tut, tut, child; mustn't despise small things!"

"Such as Mr. Greenwood," said Polly irrepressibly, "weight two hundred and ninety pounds; and Mrs. Darling, height six feet one inch; no, I'll try not to despise small things, thank you!"

"Well, if there's a vocation, it will 'call,' you know, Polly. I'd rather like you for an assistant, to drive my horse and amuse my convalescents. Bless my soul! you'd make a superb nurse, except—"

"Except what, sir?"

"You're not in equilibrium yet, my child; you are either up or down, generally up. You bounce, so to speak. Now, a nurse mustn't bounce; she must be poised, as it were, or suspended betwixt and between, like Mahomet's coffin. But thank Heaven for your high spirits, all the same! They will tide you over many a hard place, and the years will bring the 'inevitable yoke' soon enough, Polly," and here Dr. George passed behind the girl's chair and put his two kind hands on her shoulders. "Polly, can you be really a woman? Can you put the little-girl days bravely behind you?"

"I can, Dr. George." This in a very trembling voice.

"Can you settle all these details for your mother, and assume responsibilities? Can you take her away, as if she were the child and you the mother, all at once?"

"I can!" This more firmly.

"Can you deny yourself for her, as she has for you? Can you keep cheerful and sunny? Can you hide your fears, if there should be cause for any, in your own heart? Can you be calm and strong, if—"

"No, no!" gasped Polly, dropping her head on the back of the chair and shivering like a leaf. "No, no; don't talk about fears, Dr. George. She will be better. She will be better very soon. I could not live—"

"It isn't so easy to die, my child, with plenty of warm young blood running pell-mell through your veins, and a sixteen-year-old heart that beats like a chronometer."

"I could not bear life without mamma, Dr. George!"

"A human being, made in the image of God, can bear anything, child; but I hope you won't have to meet that sorrow for many a long year yet. I will come in tomorrow and coax your mother into a full assent to my plans; meanwhile, fly home with your medicines. There was a time when you used to give my tonics at night and my sleeping draught in the morning; but I believe in you absolutely from this day."

Polly put her two slim hands in the kind doctor's, and looking up with brimming eyes into his genial face said, "Dear Dr. George, you may believe in me; indeed, indeed you may!"

Dr. George looked out of his office window, and mused as his eyes followed Polly up the shaded walk under the pepper trees.

"Oh, these young things, these young things, how one's heart yearns over them!" he sighed. "There she goes, full tilt, notwithstanding the heat; hat swinging in her hand instead of being on her pretty head; her heart bursting with fond schemes to keep that precious mother alive. It's a splendid nature, that girl's; one that is in danger of being wrecked by its own impetuosity, but one so full and rich that it is capable of bubbling over and enriching all the dull and sterile ones about it. Now, if all the money I can rake and scrape together need not go to those languid, boneless children of my languid, boneless sister-in-law, I could put that brave little girl on her feet. I think she will be able to do battle with the world so long as she has her mother for a motive-power. The question is, how will she do it without?"

IV

Good-by to Santa Barbara

————

DR. GEORGE found Mrs. Oliver too ill to be anything but reasonable. After a long talk about her own condition and Polly's future, she gave a somewhat tearful assent to all his plans for their welfare, and agreed to make the change when a suitable tenant was found for the house.

So Polly eased the anxiety that gnawed at her heart by incredible energy in the direction of housecleaning; superintending all sorts of scrubbings, polishings, and renovating of carpets with the aid of an extra Chinaman.

Each boarder in turn was asked to make a trip to the country on a certain day, and on his return found his room in spotless order; while all this time the tired mother lay quietly in her bed, knowing little or nothing of her daughter's superhuman efforts to be "good." But a month of rest worked wonders, and Mrs. Oliver finally became so like her usual delicate but energetic self that Polly almost forgot her fears, although she remitted none of her nursing and fond but rigid discipline.

At length something happened; and one glorious Saturday morning in October, Polly saddled Blanquita, the white mare which Bell Winship had left in Polly's care during her European trip, and galloped over to the Nobles' ranch in a breathless state of excitement.

Blanquita was happy too, for Polly had a light hand on the rein and a light seat in the saddle. She knew there would be a long rest at the journey's end, and that, too, under a particularly shady pepper tree; so both horse and rider were in a golden humor as they loped over the dusty road, the blue Pacific on the one hand, and the brown hills, thirsty for rain, on the other.

Polly tied Blanquita to the pepper tree, and ran up the walnut-tree avenue to the Nobles' house. There was no one in; but that was nothing unusual, since a house is chiefly useful for sleeping purposes in that lovely climate. No one on the verandas, no one in the hammocks; after seeking for some little time she came upon Margery and her mother at work in their orange-tree sitting room, Mrs. Noble with her mending basket, Margery painting as usual.

The orange-tree sitting room was merely a platform built under the trees, which in the season of blossoms shed a heavy fragrance in the warm air, and later on hung their branches of golden fruit almost into your very lap.

"Here you are!" cried Polly, plunging through the trees as she caught sight of Margery's pink dress. "You haven't any hats to swing, so please give three rousing cheers! The house is rented and a lease signed for a year!"

"That is good news, indeed!" exclaimed Mrs. Noble, laying down her needle. "And who is the tenant?"

"Whom do you suppose? Mrs. Chadwick herself! She has been getting on very nicely with the housekeeping (part of the credit belongs to me, but no one would ever believe it), and the boarders have been gradually weaned from mamma and accustomed to the new order of things, so they are tolerably content. Ah Foy also has agreed to stay, and that makes matters still more serene, since he is the best cook in Santa Barbara. Mrs. Chadwick will pay eighty-five dollars a month. Dr. George thinks we ought to get more, but mamma is so glad to have somebody whom she knows, and so relieved to feel that there will be no general breaking up, that she is glad to accept the eighty-five dollars; and I am sure that we can live in modest penury on that sum. Of course Mrs. Chadwick may weary in welldoing; or she may die; or she may even get married—though that's very unlikely, unless one of the boarders can't pay his board and wants to make it up to her in some way. Heigho! I feel like a princess, like a capitalist, like a gilded society lady!" sighed Polly, fanning herself with her hat.

"And now you and your mother will come to us for

a week or two, as you promised, won't you?" asked Mrs. Noble. "That will give you time to make your preparations comfortably."

Polly took a note from her pocket and handed it to Mrs. Noble: "Mrs. Oliver presents her compliments to Mrs. Noble, and says in this letter that we accept with pleasure Mrs. Noble's kind invitation to visit her. Said letter was not to be delivered in case Mrs. Noble omitted to renew the invitation; but as all is right, I don't mind announcing that we are coming the day after to-morrow."

"Oh, Polly, Polly! How am I ever to live without you!" sighed Margery. "First Elsie, then Bell, now you!"

"Live for your Art with a big A, Peggy, but it's not forever. By and by, when you are a successful artist and I am a successful something, in short, when we are both 'careering,' we will 'career' together in some great metropolis. Our mothers' delicate fingers, no longer sullied by the vulgar dishcloth and duster, shall glitter with priceless gems, while you and I, the humble authors of their greatness, will heap dimes on dimes until we satisfy ambition."

Mrs. Noble smiled. "I hope your 'career,' as you call it, will be one in which imagination will be of use, Polly."

"I don't really imagine all the imaginations you imagine I imagine," said Polly soberly, as she gave Mrs. Noble's hand an affectionate squeeze. "A good deal of it is 'whistling to keep my courage up.' But everything looks hopeful just now. Mamma is so much better, everybody is so kind, and do you know, I don't loathe the boarders half so much since we have rented them with the house?

> *"They grow in beauty side by side,*
> *They fill our home with glee.*

Now that I can look upon them as personal property, part of our goods and chattels, they have ceased to be disagreeable. Even Mr. Greenwood—you remember him, Margery?"

"The fat old man who calls you sprightly?"

"The very same; but he has done worse since that. To be called sprightly is bad enough, but yesterday he said that he shouldn't be surprised *if I married well—in— course—of—time!*"

Nothing but italics would convey the biting sarcasm of Polly's inflections, and no capitals in a printer's case could picture her flashing eyes, or the vigor with which she prodded the earth with her riding whip.

"I agree with him, that it is not impossible," said Mrs. Noble teasingly, after a moment of silence.

"Now, dearest Aunty Meg, don't take sides with that odious man! If, in the distant years, you ever see me on the point of marrying well, simply mention Mr. Greenwood's name to me, and I'll draw back even if I am walking up the middle aisle with an ivory prayer book in my hand!"

"Just to spite Mr. Greenwood; that would be sensible," said Margery.

"You couldn't be so calm if you had to sit at the same table with him day after day. He belongs at the second table by—by every law of his nature! But, as I was saying, now that we have rented him to Mrs. Chadwick with the rest of the furniture, and will have a percentage on him just as we do on the piano which is far more valuable, I have been able to look at him pleasantly."

"You ought to be glad that the boarders like you," said Margery reprovingly.

"They don't, as a rule; only the horrors and the elderly gentlemen approve of me. But good-by for today, Aunty Meg. Come to the gate, Peggy dear!"

The two friends walked through the orange grove, their arms wound about each other, girl-fashion. They were silent, for each was sorry to lose the other, and a remembrance of the dear old times, the unbroken circle, the peaceful schooldays and merry vacations, stole into their young hearts, together with visions of the unknown future.

As Polly untied Blanquita and gave a heroic cinch to the saddle, she gave a last searching look at Margery, and said finally, "Peggy dear, I am very sure you are blue this morning; tell your faithful old Pollykins all about it."

One word was enough for Margery in her present mood, and she burst into tears on Polly's shoulder.

"Is it Edgar again?" whispered Polly.

"Yes," she sobbed. "Father has given him three months more to stay in the university, and unless he does better he is to come home and live on the cattle ranch. Mother is heartbroken over it; for you know, Polly, that Edgar will never endure such a life; and yet, dearly as he loves books, he isn't doing well with his studies. The president has written father that he is very indolent this term and often absent from recitations; and one of the Santa Barbara boys, a senior, writes Philip that he is not choosing good friends, nor taking any rank in his class. Mother has written him such a letter this morning! If he can read it without turning his back upon his temptations, whatever they may be, I shall never have any pride in him again; and oh, Polly, I have been so proud of him, my brilliant, handsome, charming brother!"

"Poor Edgar! I can't believe it is anything that will last. He is so bright and lovable; everyone thought he would take the highest honors. Why, Margery, he is, or was, the most ambitious boy I ever knew; and surely, surely he cannot have changed altogether! Surely he will come to himself when he knows he may have to leave college unless he does his best. I'm so sorry, dear old Peggy! It seems heartless that my brighter times should begin just when you are in trouble. Perhaps mamma and I can do something for Edgar; we will try, you may be sure. Good-by, dearest; I shall see you again very soon."

Ten days later, Polly stood on the deck of the "Orizaba" just at dusk, looking back on lovely Santa Barbara as it lay in the lap of the foothills freshened by the first rains. The dull, red-tiled roofs of the old Spanish adobes gleamed through the green of the pepper trees, the tips of the tall, straggling blue gums stood out sharply against the sky, and the twin towers of the old Mission rose in dazzling whiteness above a wilderness of verdure. The friendly faces on the wharf first merged themselves into a blurred mass of moving atoms, then sank into nothingness.

Polly glanced into her stateroom. Mrs. Oliver was a good sailor, and was lying snug and warm under her blankets. So Polly took a camp-chair just outside the door, wrapped herself in her fur cape, and sat there alone as the sunset glow paled in the western sky and darkness fell upon the face of the deep.

The mesa faded from sight; and then the lighthouse, where she had passed so many happy hours in her childhood. The bright disk of flame shone clear and steady across the quiet ocean, seeming to say, *Let your light so shine! Let your light so shine! Good luck, Polly! Keep your own lamp filled and trimmed, like a wise little virgin!* And her heart answered, "Good-by, dear light! I am leaving my little-girl days on the shore with you, and I am out on the open sea of life. I shall know that you are shining, though I cannot see you. Good-by! Shine on, dear light! I am going to seek my fortune!"

V

Told in Letters

SAN FRANCISCO, November 1, 188–

DEAR MARGERY—I have been able to write you only scraps of notes heretofore, but now that we are quite settled I can tell you about our new home. We were at a hotel for a week, as long as I, the family banker, felt that we could afford it. At the end of that time, by walking the streets from morning till night, looking at every house with a sign "To Let" on it, and taking mamma to see only the desirable ones, we found a humble spot to lay our heads. It is a tiny upper flat, which we rent for thirty dollars a month. The landlady calls it furnished, but she has an imagination which takes even higher flights than mine. Still, with the help of the pretty things we brought with us, we are very cosy and comfortable. There is a tiny living room, which, with our Santa Barbara draperies, tablecovers, tea table, and books, looks like a corner of the dear home sitting room. Out of this living room is a sunny bedroom with two single beds, and space enough to spare for mamma's rocking chair in front of a window that looks out on the Golden Gate. The dining room just holds, by a squeeze, the extension-table and four chairs; and the dot of a kitchen, with a tiny gas stove, completes the suite.

We are dining at a restaurant a short distance off, at present, and I cook the breakfasts and luncheons; but on Monday, as mamma is so well, I begin school from nine to twelve each day under a special arrangement, and we are to have a little Chinese boy who will assist in the work and go home at night to sleep. I shall walk one way to school, although it is sixteen squares and all up and down hill. . . .

The rains thus far have been mostly in the night, and we have lovely days. Mamma and I take long rides on the cable cars in the afternoon, and stay out at the Cliff House on the rocks every pleasant Saturday. Then we've discovered nice sheltered nooks in the sand dunes beyond the park, and there we stay for hours, mamma reading while I study. We are so quiet and so happy; we were never alone together in our lives before. You, dear Peggy, who have always had your family to yourself, can hardly think how we enjoy being at table together, just we two. We have a few pleasant friends here, you know, and they come to see mamma without asking her to return the calls, as they see plainly she has no strength for society. . . .

POLLY.

P.S. We have a remarkable front door, which opens with a spring located in the wall at the top of the stairs. I never tire of opening it, even though each time I am obliged to go downstairs to close it again.

When Dr. George came last week, he rang the bell, and being tired with the long pull up the hill, leaned against the door to breathe. Of course I knew nothing of this, and as soon as I heard the bell I flew to open the door with my usual neatness and dispatch, when who should tumble in, full length, but poor dear Dr. George! He was so surprised, and the opposite neighbors were so interested, and I was so sorry, that I was almost hysterical. Dr. George insists that the door is a trap laid for unsuspecting country people.

November 9.

. . . The first week is over, and the finances didn't come out right at all. I have a system of bookkeeping which is original, simple, practical, and absolutely reliable. The house money I keep in a cigar box with three partitions (formerly used for birds' eggs), and I divide the month's money in four parts, and pay everything weekly.

The money for carfare, clothing, and sundries I keep in an old silver sugar bowl, and the reserve fund, which we are never to touch save on the most dreadful provocation, in a Japanese ginger jar with a cover. These, plainly marked, repose in my upper drawer. Mamma has no business cares whatever, and everything ought to work to a charm, as it will after a while. But this first week has been discouraging, and I have had to borrow enough from compartment two, cigar box, to pay debts incurred by compartment one, cigar box. This is probably because we had to buy a bag of flour and ten pounds of sugar. Of course this won't happen every week. . . .

I wrote Ah Foy a note after we arrived, for he really seems to have a real affection for us. I inclose his answer to my letter. It is such a miracle of Chinese construction that it is somewhat difficult to get his idea; still I think I see that he is grateful for past favors; that he misses us; that the boarders are going on "very happy and joy"; that he is glad mamma is better, and pleased with the teacher I selected for him. But here it is; judge for yourself.

SANTA BARBARA, November 5.

DEAR MY FREND.

I was joy pleased to received a letter from you how
are Your getting along and my Dear if your leaves a go
We but now I been it is here I am very sorry for are a
your go to in San Francisco if any now did you been
it is that here very happy and joy I am so glad for your
are to do teachers for me but I am very much thank you
dear my frend.

Good-By.   AH FOY.

November 15.

. . . The first compartment, cigar box, couldn't pay
back the money it borrowed from the second compartment, and so this in turn had to borrow from the third
compartment. I could have made everything straight,
I think, if we hadn't bought a feather duster and a gal-
lon of kerosene. The first will last forever, and the
second for six weeks, so it isn't fair to call compartment
number two extravagant. At the end of this month I
shall remove some of the partitions in the cigar box and
keep the house money in two parts, balancing accounts
every fortnight. . . .

November 24.

. . . My bookkeeping is in a frightful snarl. There is
neither borrowing nor lending in the cigar box now, for
all the money for the month is gone at the end of the
third week. The water, it seems, was not included in the
thirty dollars for the rent, and compartment three had

to pay two dollars for that purpose when compartment two was still deeply in its debt. If compartment two had only met its rightful obligations, compartment three needn't have "failed up," as they say in New England; but as it is, poor compartment four is entirely bankrupt, and will have to borrow of the sugar bowl or the ginger jar. As these banks are not at all in the same line of business, they ought not to be drawn into the complications of the cigar box, for they will have their own troubles by and by; but I don't know what else to do. . . .

December 2.

. . . It came out better at the end of the month than I feared, for we spent very little last week, and have part of the ten pounds of sugar, kerosene, feather duster, scrubbing brush, tapioca, and spices with which to begin the next month. I suffered so with the debts, losses, business embarrassments, and failures of the four compartments that when I found I was only four dollars behind on the whole month's expenses, I knocked out all the compartments, and am not going to keep things in weeks. I made up the deficit by taking two dollars out of the reserve fund, and two dollars out of my ten-dollar gold piece that Dr. George gave me on my birthday.

I have given the ginger jar an IOU for two dollars from the cigar box, and it has resumed business at the old stand. Compartment four, cigar box, which is perfectly innocent, as it was borrowed out of house and home by compartment three, also had to give a note to the sugar bowl, and I made the ginger jar give me an IOU for my two dollars birthday money.

Whether all these obligations will be met without lawsuits, I cannot tell; but I know by the masterly manner in which I have fought my way through these intricate affairs with the loss of only four dollars in four weeks, that I possess decided business ability, and this gives me courage to struggle on.

December 30, 188–.

. . . We are having hard times, dear old Margery, though I do not regret coming to San Francisco, for mamma could not bear the slightest noise or confusion, nor lift her hand to any sort of work, in her present condition. At any rate, we came by Dr. George's orders, so my conscience is clear. . . .

Mrs. Chadwick has sent us only sixty-five dollars this month, instead of eighty-five. Some of the boarders are behind in their payments. The Darlings have gone away, and "she hopes to do better next month." Mamma cannot bear to press her, she is so kind and well-meaning; so do not for the world mention the matter to Dr. George. I will write to him when I must, not before.

Meanwhile I walk to school both ways, saving a dollar and a quarter a month. Have found a cheaper laundry; one dollar more saved. Cut down fruit bill; one dollar more. Blacked my white straw sailor with shoe-blacking, trimmed it with a white ribbon; result perfectly hideous, but the sugar bowl, clothing, and sundry fund are out of debt and doing well. Had my faded gray dress dyed black, and trimmed the jacket with pieces of my moth-eaten cock's-feather boa; perfectly elegant, almost too gorgeous for my humble circumstances. Mamma looks at me sadly when I don these ancient garments, and almost wishes I hadn't such "a wealthy look." I tell her I expect the girls to say, when I walk into the school yard on Monday, "Who is this that cometh with dyed garments from Bozrah?"

Mamma has decided that I may enter a training school for kindergartners next year; so I am taking the studies that will give me the best preparation, and I hope to earn part of my tuition fees, when the time comes, by teaching as assistant. . . .

I go over to Berkeley once a week to talk Spanish with kind Professor Salazar and his wife. They insist that it is a pleasure, and will not allow mamma to pay anything for the lessons. I also go every Tuesday to tell stories at the Children's Hospital. It is the dearest hour of the week. When I am distracted about bills and expenses and mamma's health and Mrs. Chadwick's mismanagements and Yung Lee's mistakes (for he is beautiful as an angel and stupid as a toad), I put on my hat and go out to the children, poor little things! They always have a welcome for me, bless them! and I always come back ready to take up my trials again. Edgar is waiting to take this to the postbox, so I must say good night. He is such a pleasure to us and such a comfort to mamma. I know for the first time in my life the fun of having a brother.

Ever your affectionate   POLLYKINS.

118   POLLY OLIVER'S PROBLEM

The foregoing extracts from Polly's business letters
give you an idea only of her financial difficulties. She
was tempted to pour these into one sympathizing ear,
inasmuch as she kept all annoyances from her mother
as far as possible; though household economies, as devised by her, lost much of their terror.

Mrs. Oliver was never able to see any great sorrow
in a monthly deficit when Polly seated herself before
her cash boxes and explained her highly original financial operations. One would be indeed in dire distress of
mind could one refrain from smiling when, having
made the preliminary announcement—"The great fem-
inine financier of the century is in her counting room:
let the earth tremble!"—she planted herself on the bed,
oriental fashion, took pencil and account book in lap,
spread cigar box, sugar bowl, and ginger jar before her
on the pillows, and ruffled her hair for the approaching
contest.

VI

A Little Missionary Work

ONE CHANGE had come over their life during these months which, although not explained in Polly's correspondence, concerns our little circle of people very intimately.

The Olivers had been in San Francisco over a month, but though Edgar Noble had been advised of the fact, he had not come over from Berkeley to see his old friends. Polly had at length written him a note, which still remained unanswered when she started one afternoon on a trip across the bay for her first Spanish conversation with Professor Salazar. She had once visited the university buildings, but Professor Salazar lived not only at some distance from the college, but at some distance from everything else. Still, she had elaborate written directions in her pocket, and hoped to find the place without difficulty.

She had no sooner alighted at the station than she felt an uneasy consciousness that it was not the right one, and that she should have gone farther before leaving the railway. However, there was no certainty about it in her mind, so after asking at two houses half a mile apart, and finding that the inmates had never heard of Professor Salazar's existence, she walked down a shady road, hoping to find another household where his name and fame had penetrated.

The appointed hour for the lessons was half past three on Fridays, but it was after four, and Polly seemed to be walking farther and farther away from civilization.

"I shall have to give it up," she thought. "I will go back to the station where I got off and wait until the next train for San Francisco comes along, which will be nobody knows when. How provoking it is, and how stupid I am! Professor Salazar will stay at home for me, and very likely Mrs. Salazar has made butter cakes and coffee, and here am I floundering in the woods! I'll sit down under these trees and do a bit of Spanish, while I'm resting for the walk back."

Just at this moment a chorus of voices sounded in the distance, then some loud talking, then more singing.

"It is some of the students," thought Polly, and decided to stay behind her tree until they should pass.

But they did not pass. Just as they came opposite her

hiding place, they threw themselves down in a sunny spot on the opposite side of the road and lighted their cigarettes.

"No hurry!" said one. "Let's take it easy; the train doesn't leave till 4:50. Where are you going, Ned?"

"Home, I suppose, where I was going when you met me. I told you I could only walk to the turn."

"Home? No, you don't!" expostulated half a dozen laughing voices; "we've unearthed the would-be hermit, and we're going to keep him."

"Can't go with you tonight, boys, worse luck!" repeated the second speaker. "Got to cram for that examination or be plucked again; and one more plucking will settle this child's university career!"

"Oh, let the examinations go to the dickens! What's the use?—all the same a hundred years hence. The idea of cramming on a Friday night! Come on!"

"Can't do it, fellows; but next time goes. See you Monday. Ta-ta!"

Polly peeped cautiously from behind her tree.

"I believe that voice is Edgar Noble's, or else I'm very much mistaken. I thought of it when I first heard them singing. Yes, it is! Now, those hateful boys are going to get him into trouble!"

Just at this moment four of the boys jumped from the ground and, singing vociferously—

> *"He won't go home any more,*
> *He won't go home any more,*
> *He won't go home any more,*
> *Way down on the Bingo farm!"*

rushed after young Noble, pinioned him, and brought him back.

"See here, Noble," expostulated one of them, who seemed to be a commanding genius among the rest—"see here, don't go and be a spoil-sport! What's the matter with you? We're going to chip in for a good dinner, go to a show, and then—oh, then we'll go and have a game of billiards. You play so well that you won't lose anything. And if you want money, Will's flush, he'll lend you a tenner. You know there won't be any fun in it unless you're there! We'll get the last boat back to-night, or the first in the morning."

A letter from his mother lay in Edgar's pocket—a letter which had brought something like tears to his eyes for a moment, and over which he had vowed better things. But he yielded, nevertheless—that it was with reluctance didn't do any particular good to anybody, though the recording angels may have made a note of it—and strolled along with the other students, who were evidently in great glee over their triumph.

Meanwhile Polly had been plotting. Her brain was not a great one, but it worked very swiftly; Dr. George called it, chaffingly, a small mind in a very active state. Scarcely stopping to think, lest her courage should not be equal to the strain of meeting six or eight young men face to face, she stepped softly out of her retreat, walked gently down the road, and when she had come within ten feet of the group, halted, and, clearing her throat desperately, said, "I beg your pardon—"

The whole party turned with one accord, a good deal

of amazement in their eyes, as there had not been a sign of life on the road a moment before, and now here was a sort of woodland sprite, a "nut-brown maid," with a remarkably sweet voice.

"I beg your pardon, but can you tell me the way to Professor Salazar's house? Why" (this with a charming smile and expression as of one having found an angel of deliverance),—"why, it is—isn't it?—Edgar Noble of Santa Barbara!"

Edgar, murmuring, "Polly Oliver, by Jove!" lifted his hat at once, and saying, "Excuse me, boys," turned back and gallantly walked at Polly's side.

"Why, Miss Polly, this is an unexpected way of meeting you!"

("Very unexpected," thought Polly.) "Is it not, indeed? I wrote you a note the other day, telling you that we hoped to see you soon in San Francisco."

"Yes," said Edgar, "I didn't answer it because I intended to present myself in person tomorrow or Sunday. What are you doing in this vicinity?" he continued.

"No wonder you ask. I am 'floundering,' at present. I came over to a Spanish lesson at Professor Salazar's, and I have quite lost my way. If you will be kind enough to put me on the right road I shall be very much obliged, though I don't like to keep you from your friends," said Polly with a quizzical smile. "You see, the professor won't know why I missed my appointment, and I can't bear to let him think me capable of neglect; he has been so very kind."

"But you can't walk there. You must have gotten off at the wrong station; it is quite a mile, even across the fields."

"And what is a mile, sir? Have you forgotten that I am a country girl?" and she smiled up at him brightly, with a look that challenged remembrance.

"I remember that you could walk with any of us," said Edgar, thinking how the freckles had disappeared from Polly's roseleaf skin, and how particularly fetching she looked in her brown felt hat. "Well, if you really wish to go there, I'll see you safely to the house and take you over to San Francisco afterward, as it will be almost dark. I was going over, at any rate, and one train earlier or later won't make any difference."

("Perhaps it won't and perhaps it will," thought Polly.) "If you are sure it won't be too much trouble, then—"

"Not a bit. Excuse me a moment while I run back and explain the matter to the boys."

The boys did not require any elaborate explanation. Oh, the power of a winsome face! No better than many other good things, but surely one of them, and when it is united to a fair amount of goodness, something to be devoutly thankful for. It is to be feared that if a lumpish, dumpish sort of girl (good as gold, you know, but not suitable for occasions when a fellow's will has to be caught "on the fly," and held until it settles to its work),—if that lumpish, dumpish girl had asked the way to Professor Salazar's house, Edgar Noble would have led her courteously to the turn of the road, lifted his hat, and wished her a pleasant journey.

But Polly was wearing her Sunday dress of brown cloth and a jaunty jacket trimmed with fur (the best bits of an old coat of Mrs. Oliver's). The sun shone on the loose-dropping coil of the waving hair that was only caught in place by a tortoise-shell comb; the wind blew some of the dazzling tendrils across her forehead; the eyes that glanced up from under her smart little hat were as blue as sapphires; and Edgar, as he looked, suddenly feared that there might be vicious bulls in the meadows, and didn't dare as a gentleman to trust Polly alone! He hadn't remembered anything special about her, but after an interval of two years she seemed all at once as desirable as dinner, as tempting as the show, almost as fascinating as the billiards, when one has just money enough in one's pocket for one's last week's bills and none at all for the next!

The boys, as I say, had imagined Edgar's probable process of reasoning. Polly was standing in the high-road, and when Edgar explained that it was his duty to see her safely to her destination, they all bowed to the inevitable. The one called Tony even said that he would be glad to "swap" with him, and the whole party offered to support him in his escort duty if he said the word. He agreed to meet the boys later, as Polly's quick ear assured her, and having behaved both as a man of honor and knight of chivalry, he started unsuspectingly across the fields with his would-be guardian.

She darted a searching look at him as they walked along.

"Oh, how old and 'gentlemanly' you look, Edgar! I feel quite afraid of you!"

"Polly, shall I tell you the truth?" said Edgar

"I'm glad you do. There used to be a painful lack of reverence in your manners, Miss Polly."

"There used to be a painful lack of politeness in yours, Mr. Edgar. Oh dear, I meant to begin so nicely with you and astonish you with my new grown-up manners! Now, Edgar, let us begin as if we had just been introduced; if you will try your best not to be provoking, I won't say a single disagreeable thing."

"Polly, shall I tell you the truth?"

"You might try; it would be good practice even if you didn't accomplish anything."

"How does that remark conform with your late promises? However, I'll be forgiving and see if I receive any reward; I've tried every other line of action. What I was going to say when you fired that last shot was this: I agree with Jack Howard, who used to say that he would rather quarrel with you than be friends with any other girl."

"It is nice," said Polly complacently. "I feel a sort of pleasant glow myself, whenever I've talked to you a few minutes; but the trouble is that you used to fan that pleasant glow into a raging heat, and then we both got angry."

"If the present 'raging heat' has faded into the 'pleasant glow,' I don't mind telling you that you are very much improved," said Edgar encouragingly. "Your temper seems much the same, but no one who knew you at fourteen could have foreseen that you would turn out so exceedingly well."

"Do you mean that I am better looking?" asked Polly, with the excited frankness of sixteen years.

"Exactly."

"Oh, thank you, thank you, Edgar. I'm a thousand times obliged. I've thought so myself, lately; but it's worth everything to have your grown-up, college opinion. Of course red hair has come into vogue, that's one point in my favor, though I fear mine is a little vivid even for the fashion; Margery has done a water color of my head which Phil says looks like the explosion of a tomato. Then my freckles are almost gone, and that is a great help; if you examine me carefully in this strong light you can only count seven, and two of those are getting fainthearted. Nothing can be done with my aspiring nose. I've tried in vain to push it down, and now I'm simply living it down."

Edgar examined her in the strong light mischievously. "Turn your profile," he said. "That's right; now, do you know, I rather like your nose, and it's a very valuable index to your disposition. I don't know whether, if it were removed from your face, it would mean so much; but taken in connection with its surroundings, it's a very expressive feature; it warns the stranger to be careful. In fact, most of your features are danger signals, Polly; I'm rather glad I've been taking a course in First Aid!"

And so, with a great deal of nonsense and a good sprinkling of quiet, friendly chat, they made their way to Professor Salazar's house, proffered Polly's apologies, and took the train for San Francisco.

VII

"*Where Ignorance Is Bliss*"

———

THE TRIP from Berkeley to San Francisco was a brilliant success from Edgar's standpoint, but Polly would have told you that she never worked harder in her life.

"I'll just say 'How do you do?' to your mother, and then be off," said Edgar, as they neared the house.

"Oh, but you surely will stay to dinner with us!" said Polly with the most innocent look of disappointment on her face—a look of such obvious grief that a person of any feeling could hardly help wishing to remove it, if possible. "You see, Edgar" (putting the latch-key in the door), "mamma is so languid and ill that she cannot indulge in many pleasures, and I had quite counted on you to amuse her a little for me this evening. But come up, and you shall do as you like after dinner.

"I've brought you a surprise, mamma!" called Polly from the stairs, "an old friend whom I picked up in the woods like a wild flower and brought home to you." ("Wild flower is a good name for him," she thought.)

Mrs. Oliver was delighted to see Edgar, but after the first greetings were over, Polly fancied that she had not closed the front door, and Edgar offered to go down and make sure.

In a second Polly crossed the room to her mother's side, and whispered impressively, "Edgar *must* be kept here until after midnight; I have good reasons that I will explain when we are alone. Keep him somehow—anyhow!"

Mrs. Oliver had not lived sixteen years with Polly without learning to leap to conclusions. "Run down and ask Mrs. Howe if she will let us have her hall bedroom tonight," she replied, "nod your head for *yes* when you come back, and I'll act accordingly; I have a request to make of Edgar, and am glad to have so early an opportunity of talking with him."

"We did close the door, after all," said Edgar, coming in again. "What a pretty little apartment you have here! I haven't seen anything so cozy and homelike for ages."

"Then make yourself at home in it," said Mrs. Oliver, while Polly joined in with, "Isn't that a pretty fire in the grate? I'll give you one rose-colored lamp with your firelight. Here, mamma, is the rocker for you on one side; here, Edgar, is our one 'man's chair' for you on the other. Stretch out your feet as lazily as you like on my new goatskin rug. You are our only home friend in San

Francisco; and oh, how mamma will spoil you whenever she has the chance! Now talk to each other cozily while the 'angel of the house' cooks dinner."

It may be mentioned here that as Mrs. Chadwick's monthly remittances varied from sixty to seventy-five dollars, but never reached the promised eighty-five, Polly had dismissed little Yung Lee for a month, two weeks of which would be the Christmas vacation, and hoped in this way to make up deficiencies. The sugar bowl and ginger jar were stuffed copiously with IOU's signed "Cigar box," but held a painfully small amount of cash.

"Can't I go out and help Polly?" asked Edgar, a little later. "I should never have agreed to stay and dine if I had known that she was the cook."

"Go out, by all means; but you needn't be anxious. Ours is a sort of doll-housekeeping. We buy everything cooked, as far as possible, and Polly makes play of the rest. It all seems so simple and interesting to plan for two when we have been used to twelve and fourteen."

"May I come in?" called Edgar from the tiny dining room to Polly, who had laid aside her Sunday finery and was clad in brown Scotch gingham mostly covered with ruffled apron.

"Yes, if you like; but you won't be spoiled here, so don't hope it. Mamma and I are two very different persons. Tie that apron round your waist; I've just begun the salad dressing; is your intelligence equal to stirring it round and round and pouring in oil drop by drop, while I take up the dinner?"

"Fully. Just try me. I'll make it stand on its head!"

Meanwhile Polly set on the table a platter of lamb chops, some delicate potato chips which had come out of a pasteboard box, a dish of canned French peas, and a mound of currant jelly.

"That is good," she remarked critically, coming back to her apprentice, who was toiling with most unnecessary vigor, so that the veins stood out boldly on his forehead. "You're really not stupid, for a boy; and you haven't 'made a mess,' which is more than I hoped. Now, please pour the dressing over those sliced tomatoes; set them on the side table in the banquet hall; put the plate in the sink (don't stare at me!); open a bottle of Apollinaris for mamma—dig out the cork with a hairpin, I've lost the corkscrew; move three chairs up to the dining table (oh, it's such fun to have three!); light the silver candlesticks in the center of the table; go in and bring mamma out in style; see if the fire needs coal; and I'll be ready by that time."

"I can never remember, but I fly! Oh, what an excellent slavedriver was spoiled in you!" said Edgar.

The simple dinner was delicious, and such a welcome change from the long boarding-house table at which Edgar had eaten for over a year. The candles gave a soft light; there was a bowl of yellow flowers underneath them. Mrs. Oliver looked like an elderly Dresden-china shepherdess in her pale blue wrapper, and Polly didn't suffer from the brown gingham, with its wide collar and cuffs of bluff embroidery, and its quaint full sleeves. She had burned two small blisters on her wrist; they were scarcely visible to the naked eye, but she

succeeded in obtaining as much sympathy for them as
if they had been mortal wounds. Her mother murmured 'Poor darling wrist.' Edgar found a bit of thin
cambric and bound up the injured member with cool-
ing flour, Mistress Polly looking demurely on, thinking
meanwhile how much safer he was with them than
with the objectionable Tony. After the lamb chops and
peas had been discussed, Edgar insisted on changing
the plates and putting on the tomato salad; then Polly
officiated at the next course, bringing in coffee, sliced
oranges, and delicious cake from the neighboring bakery.

"Can't I wash the dishes?" asked Edgar, when the
feast was ended.

"They are not going to be washed, at least by us.
This is a great occasion, and the little girl downstairs
is coming up to clear away the dinner things."

Then there was the pleasant living room again, and
when the candles were lighted in the old-fashioned mirror over the fireplace, everything wore a festive appearance. The guitar was brought out, and Edgar sang college songs till Mrs. Oliver grew so bright that she even
hummed a faint second from her cozy place on the sofa.

By this time the bandage had come off the burned
wrist, and Edgar must bind it on again, and Polly
shrieked and started when he pinned the end over, and
Edgar turned pale at the thought of his brutal awk-
wardness, and Polly burst into a ringing peal of laughter and confessed that the pin hadn't touched her, and
Edgar called her a deceitful little wretch. This natu-

rally occupied some time, and soon it was nearly eleven o'clock, but up to this time Edgar had shown no realizing sense of his engagements.

"The dinner is over, and the theatre party is safe," thought Polly. "Now comes the 'tug of war,' that mysterious game of billiards."

But Mrs. Oliver was equal to the occasion. When Edgar looked at his watch, she said: "Polly, run and get Mrs. Noble's last letter, dear"; and then, when she was alone with Edgar, "My dear boy, I have a favor to ask of you, and you must be quite frank if it is not convenient for you to grant it. As tomorrow will be Saturday, perhaps you have no recitations, and if not, would it trouble you too much to stay here all night and attend to something for me in the morning? I will explain the matter, and then you can answer me more decidedly. I have received a letter from a Washington friend who seems to think it possible that a pension may be granted to me. He sends a letter of introduction to General M——, at the Presidio, who, he says, knew Colonel Oliver, and will be able to advise me in the matter. I am not well enough to go there for some days, and of course I do not like to send Polly alone. If you could go out with her, give him the letter of introduction, and ask him kindly to call upon us at his leisure, and find out also if there is any danger in a little delay just now while I am ill, it would be a very great favor."

"Of course I will, with all the pleasure in life, Mrs. Oliver," replied Edgar, with the unspoken thought: "Confound it! There goes my game; I promised the fellows to be there, and they'll laugh at me for staying away! However, there's nothing else to do. I shouldn't have the face to go out now and come in at one or two o'clock in the morning."

Polly entered just then with the letter.

"Edgar is going to be kind enough to stay all night with us, dear, and take you to the Presidio on the pension business in the morning. If you will see that his room is all right, I will say good night now. Our guest room is downstairs, Edgar; I hope you will be very comfortable. Breakfast at half past eight, please."

When the door of Mrs. Howe's bedroom closed on Edgar, Polly ran upstairs and sank exhausted on her own bed.

"Now, mamma, listen to my tale of woe! I got off at the wrong station—yes, it was stupid, but wait: perhaps I was led to be stupid. I lost my way, couldn't find Professor Salazar's house, couldn't find anything else. As I sat down to rest under a tree, I heard a crowd of boys singing vociferously as they came along the road. It turned out to be half a dozen university students, and at first I didn't know that Edgar was among them. They were teasing somebody to go over to San Francisco for a dinner, then to a show, and then to wind up with a game of billiards, and other gaieties which were to be prolonged indefinitely. What dreadful things may have been included I don't know. A wretch named 'Tony' did most of the teasing, and he looked equal to planning any sort of mischief. All at once I thought I recognized a familiar voice. I peeped out, and sure enough it was Edgar Noble whom they were coaxing. He didn't want to go a bit—I'll say that for him—but they were determined that he should. I didn't mind his going to dinner and a show, of course, but when they spoke of being out until after midnight, or tomorrow morning, and when one beetle-browed, vulgar-looking creature offered to lend him a 'tenner,' I thought of the mortgage on the Noble ranch, and the trouble there would be if Edgar should get into debt, and I felt I must do something to stop him, especially as he said himself that everything depended on his next examinations."

"But how did you accomplish it?" asked Mrs. Oliver, sitting up in bed and glowing with interest.

"They sat down by the roadside, smoking and talking it over. There wasn't another well-bred looking young man in the group. Edgar seemed a prince among them, and I was so ashamed of him for having such friends! I was afraid they would stay there until dark, but they finally got up and walked toward the station. I waited a few moments, went softly along behind them, and when I was near enough I cleared my throat and said, 'I beg your pardon, but can you direct me to Professor Salazar's house?' and then in a dramatic tone, 'Why, it is—isn't it?—Edgar Noble of Santa Barbara!' He joined me, of course. Oh, I can't begin to tell you all the steps of the affair, I am so exhausted. Anyway, he walked to Professor Salazar's with me to make my excuses, came over to town with me, came up to the house, I trembling for fear he would slip through my fingers at any moment; then, you know, he stayed to dinner, I in terror all the time as the fatal hours approached and departed; and there he is, tucked up in

Mrs. Howe's best bed, thanks to your ingenuity! I could never have devised that last plot, mamma; it was a masterpiece!"

"You did a kind deed, little daughter," said Mrs. Oliver, with a kiss. "But poor Mrs. Noble! What can we do for her? We cannot play policemen all the time. We are too far from Edgar to know his plans, and any interference of which he was conscious would be worse than nothing. I cannot believe that he is far wrong yet. He certainly never appeared better; so polite and thoughtful and friendly. Well, we must let the morrow bring counsel."

"I hope that smirking, odious Tony is disappointed!" said Polly viciously, as she turned out the light. "I distinctly heard him tell Edgar to throw a handkerchief over my hair if we should pass any wild cattle! How I'd like to banish him from this vicinity! Invite Edgar to dinner next week, mamma, not too soon, or he will suspect missionary work. Boys hate to be missionaried, and I'm sure I don't blame them. I hope he is happy downstairs in his little prison! He ought to be, if ignorance is bliss!"

VIII

Two Fireside Chats

———

It was five o'clock Saturday afternoon, and Edgar Noble stood on the Olivers' steps, Mrs. Oliver waving her hand from an upper window, and Polly standing on the stairs saying good-by.

"Come over to dinner some night, won't you, Edgar?" she asked carelessly, "any night you like, Wednesday, Thursday, Friday."

"Wednesday, please, it comes first!" said Edgar roguishly. "May I help cook it?"

"You not only may, but you must. Good-by."

Polly went upstairs, and, after washing the lunch dishes in a reflective turn of mind which did away with part of the irksomeness of the task, went into the living room and sat on a stool at her mother's feet.

A soft rain had begun to fall; the fire burned brightly;

138

the bamboo cast feathery shadows on the wall; from a house across the street came the sound of a beautiful voice singing:

"Oh, holy night! the stars are brightly shining.
It is the night of the dear Saviour's birth!"

All was peaceful and homelike; if it would only last, thought Polly.

"You are well tonight, mamacita."

A look of repressed pain crossed Mrs. Oliver's face as she smoothed the bright head lying in her lap. "Very comfortable, dear, and very happy; as who would not be, with such a darling comfort of a daughter? Always sunny, always helpful, these last dear weeks—cook, housekeeper, nurse, banker, all in one, with never a complaint as one burden after another is laid on her willing shoulders."

"Don't, mamma!" whispered Polly, seeking desperately for her handkerchief. "I can stand scolding, but compliments always make me cry; you know they do. If Ferdinand and Isabella had told Columbus to discover my handkerchief instead of America, he wouldn't have been as famous as he is now; there, I've found it. Now, mamma, you know your whole duty is to be well, well, well, and I'll take care of everything else."

"I've been thinking about Edgar, Polly, and I have a plan, but I shall not think of urging it against your will; you are the mistress of the house nowadays."

"I know what it is," sighed Polly. "You think we ought to take another boarder. A desire for boarders is like a taste for strong drink; once acquired, it is almost impossible to eradicate it from the system."

"I do think we ought to take this boarder. Not because it will make a difference in our income, but I am convinced that if Edgar can have a pleasant home and our companionship just at this juncture, he will break away from his idle habits, and perhaps his bad associations, and take a fresh start. I feel that we owe it to our dear old friends to do this for them, if we can. Of course, if it proves too great a tax upon you, or if I should have another attack of illness, it will be out of the question; but who knows? perhaps two or three months will accomplish our purpose. He can pay me whatever he has been paying in Berkeley, less the amount of his fare to and fro. We might have little Yung Lee again, and Mrs. Howe will be glad to rent her extra room. It has a fireplace, and will serve for both bedroom and study, if we add a table and student lamp."

"I don't believe he will come," said Polly. "We are all very well as a diversion, but as a constancy we should pall upon him. I never could keep up to the level I have been maintaining for the last twenty-four hours, that is certain. It is nothing short of degradation to struggle as hard to amuse a boy as I have struggled to amuse Edgar. I don't believe he could endure such exhilaration week after week, and I am very sure it would kill me. Besides, he will fancy he is going to be watched and reported at headquarters in Santa Barbara!"

"I think very likely you are right; but perhaps I can put the matter so that it will strike him in some other light."

"Very well, mamma, I'm resigned. It will break up

all our nice little two-ing, but we will be his guardian
angel. I will be his guardian and you his angel, and oh,
how he would dislike it if he knew it! But wait until
odious Mr. Tony meets him tonight! What business is
it of his if my hair *is* red! When he teases him for breaking his appointment, I dare say we shall never see him
again."

"You are so jolly comfortable here! This house is the
next best thing to mother," said Edgar, with boyish
heartiness, as he stood on the white goatskin with his
back to the Olivers' cheerful fireplace.

It was Wednesday evening of the next week. Polly
was clearing away the dinner things, and Edgar had
been arranging Mrs. Oliver's chair and pillows and
footstool like the gentle young knight he was by nature.

What wonder that all the fellows, even "smirking
Tony," liked him and sought his company? He who
could pull an oar, throw a ball, leap a bar, ride a horse,
or play a game of skill as if he had been born for each
particular occupation—what wonder that the ne'er-do-
wells and idlers and scamps and dullards battered at
his door continually and begged him to leave his books
and come out and "stir up things"!

"If you think it is so jolly," said Mrs. Oliver, "how
would you like to come here and live with us awhile?"

This was a bombshell. The boy hesitated, naturally,
being taken quite by surprise. ("Confound it!" he
thought rapidly, "how shall I get out of this scrape
without being impolite! They wouldn't give me one

night out a week if I came!") "I'd like it immensely, you know," he said aloud, "and it's awfully kind of you to propose it, and I appreciate it, but I don't think—I don't see, that is, how I could come, Mrs. Oliver. In the first place, I'm quite sure my family would dislike my intruding on your privacy; and then—well, you know I am out in the evening occasionally, and shouldn't like to disturb you; besides, I'm sure Miss Polly has her hands full now."

"Of course you would be often out in the evening, though I don't suppose you are a midnight reveler. You would simply have a key and go out and come in as you liked. Mrs. Howe's room is very pleasant, as you know; and you could study there before your open fire, and join us when you felt like it. Is it as convenient and pleasant for you to live on this side of the bay, and go back and forth?"

"Oh yes! I don't mind that part of it." ("This is worse than the Inquisition; I don't know but that she will get me in spite of everything!")

"Oh dear!" thought Mrs. Oliver, "he doesn't want to come; and I don't want him to come, and I must urge him to come against his will. How very disagreeable missionary work is, to be sure! I sympathize with him, too. He is afraid of petticoat government, and fears that he will lose some of his precious liberty."

"Besides, dear Mrs. Oliver," continued Edgar, after an awkward pause, "I don't think you are strong enough to have me here. I believe you're only proposing it for my good. You know that I'm in a forlorn students' boarding house, and you are anxious to give me all the comforts of a home for my mother's sake, regardless of your own discomforts."

"Come here a moment and sit beside me on Polly's footstool. You were nearly three years old when Polly was born. You were all staying with me that summer. Did you know that you were my first boarders? You were a tiny fellow in rompers, very much interested in the new baby, and very anxious to hold her. I can see you now rocking the cradle as gravely as a man. Polly has hard times and many sorrows before her, Edgar! You are old enough to see that I cannot stay with her much longer."

Edgar was too awed and too greatly moved to answer.

"I should be very glad to have you with us, both because I think we could in some degree take the place of your mother and Margery, and because I should be glad to feel that in any sudden emergency, which I do not in the least expect, we should have a near friend to lean upon ever so little."

Edgar's whole heart went out in a burst of sympathy and manly tenderness. In that moment he felt willing to give up every personal pleasure, if he might lift a feather's weight of care from the fragile woman who spoke to him with such sweetness and trust. For there is nothing hopeless save meanness and poverty of nature; and any demand on Edgar Noble's instinct of chivalrous protection would never be discounted.

"I will come gladly, gladly, Mrs. Oliver," he said, "if only I can be of service; though I fear it will be all the other way. Please borrow me for a son, just to keep me in training, and I'll try to bear my honors worthily."

"Thank you, dear boy. Then it is settled, if you are sure that the living in the city will not interfere with your studies; that is the main thing. We all look to you to add fresh laurels to your old ones. Are you satisfied with your college life thus far?"

("They haven't told her anything. That's good," thought Edgar.) "Oh yes; fairly well. I don't—I don't go in for being a grind, Mrs. Oliver. I shall never be the valedictorian, and all that sort of thing; it doesn't pay. Who ever hears of valedictorians twenty years after graduation? Class honors don't amount to much."

"I suppose they can be overestimated, but they must prove some sort of excellence which will stand one in good stead in after years. I should never advise a boy or girl to work for honors alone; but if after doing one's very best the honors come naturally, they are very pleasant."

"Half the best scholars in our class are prigs," said Edgar discontentedly. "Always down on the fellows who want some fun. Sometimes I wish I had never gone to college at all. Unless you deny yourself every pleasure, and live the life of a hermit, you can't take any rank. My father expects me to get a hundred and one per cent in every study, and thinks I ought to rise with the lark and go to bed with the chickens. I don't know whether he ever sowed any wild oats; if he did, it was so long ago that he has quite forgotten I must sow mine some time. He ought to be thankful they are such a harmless sort."

"I don't understand boys very well," said Mrs. Oliver

smilingly. "You see, I never have had any to study, and you must teach me a few things. Now, about this matter of wild oats. Why is it so necessary that they should be sown? Is Margery sowing hers? I don't know that Polly feels bound to sow any."

"I dare say they are not necessities," laughed Edgar, coloring. "Perhaps they are only luxuries."

Mrs. Oliver looked at the fire soberly. "I know there may be plenty of fine men who have a discreditable youth to look back upon—a youth finally repented of and atoned for; but that is rather a weary process, I should think, and they are surely no stronger men *because* of the 'wild oats,' but rather in *spite* of them."

"I suppose so," sighed Edgar, "but it's so easy for women to be good! I know you were born a saint, to begin with. You don't know what it is to be in college, and to want to do everything that you can't and oughtn't, and nothing that you can and ought, and get all tangled up in things you never meant to touch. However, we'll see!"

Polly peeped in at the door very softly. "They haven't any light; that's favorable. He's sitting on my footstool; he needn't suppose he is going to have *that* place! I think she has her hand on his arm—yes, she has! And he is stroking it! Oh, you poor innocent child, you do not realize that that soft little hand of my mother's never lets go! It slips into a five and three-quarters glove, but you'll be surprised, Mr. Edgar, when you discover you cannot get away from it. Very well, then; it is settled. I'll go back and put the salt fish in soak for my boarder's breakfast. I seem to have my hands rather full!—a house to keep, an invalid mother, and now a boarder. The very thing I vowed that I never would have—another boarder; what grandmamma would have called an 'unstiddy' boy boarder!"

And as Polly clattered the pots and pans, the young heathen in the parlor might have heard her fresh voice singing with great energy:

> "Shall we, whose souls are lighted
> With wisdom from on high—
> Shall we to men benighted
> The lamp of life deny?"

IX

Hard Times

———

THE NEW arrangement worked exceedingly well.

As to Edgar's innermost personal feelings, no one is qualified to speak with any authority. Whether he experienced a change of heart, vowed better things, prayed to be delivered from temptation, or simply decided to turn over a new leaf, no one knows; the principal fact in his life, at this period, seems to have been an unprecedented lack of time for any great foolishness.

Certain unpleasant things had transpired on that eventful Friday night when he had missed his appointment with his fellow-students, which had resulted in an open scandal too disagreeable to be passed over by the college authorities; the redoubtable Tony had been returned with thanks to his fond parents in a distant part of the state, and two others had been temporarily suspended.

Edgar Noble was not too blind to see the happy chance that interfered with his presence on that occasion, and was sensible enough to realize that, had he been implicated in the least degree (he scorned the possibility of his taking any active part in such scurrilous proceedings), he would probably have shared Tony's fate.

Existence was wearing a particularly dismal aspect on that afternoon when Edgar had met Polly Oliver in the Berkeley woods. He felt "nagged," injured, blue, out of sorts with fate. He had not done anything very bad, he said to himself; at least, nothing half so bad as lots of other fellows, and yet everybody frowned on him. His father had, in his opinion, been unnecessarily severe; while his mother and sister had wept over him (by letter) as if he were a thief and a forger, instead of a fellow who was simply having a little fling. He was annoyed at the conduct of Scott Burton—"king of snobs and prigs," he named him—who had taken it upon himself to inform Philip Noble of his (Edgar's) own personal affairs; and he was enraged at being preached at by that said younger brother.

But of late everything had taken an upward turn, and by way of variety, existence turned a smiling face toward him. He had passed his examinations, most unexpectedly to himself, with a respectable percentage to spare. There was a time when he would have been ashamed of this meager result. He was now, just a little,

but the feeling was somewhat submerged in his gratitude at having "squeaked through" at all.

A certain inspired Professor Hope, who wondered
what effect encouragement would have on a fellow
who didn't deserve any, but might possibly need it,
came up to him after recitations, one day, and said:

"Noble, I want to congratulate you on your papers
in history and physics. They show signal ability. There
is a plentiful lack of study evinced, but no want of
grasp or power. You have talents that ought to put you
among the first three men in the university, sir. I do
not know whether you care to take the trouble to win
such a place (it *is* a good deal of trouble), but you can
win it if you like. That's all I have to say, Noble. Good
morning!"

This unlooked-for speech fell like balm on Edgar's
wounded self-respect, and made him hold his head
higher for a week; and, naturally, while his head occupied this elevated position, he was obliged to live up
to it. He also felt obliged to make an effort, rather re-
luctantly, to maintain some decent standing in the
classes of Professor Hope, even if he shirked in all the
rest.

And now life, on the whole, save for one carking
care that perched on his shoulder by day and sat on his
eyelids at night, was very pleasant; though he could not
flatter himself that he was absolutely a free agent.

After all ordinary engagements of concerts, theatres,
lectures, or what not, he entered the house undis-
turbed, and noiselessly sought his couch. But one night,
when he ventured to stay out till well after midnight,

just as he was stealing in softly, Mrs. Oliver's gentle voice came from the head of the stairs, saying, "Good night, Edgar, the lamp is lighted in your room!"

Edgar closed his door and sat down disconsolately on the bed, his hat on the back of his head. The fire had burned to a few glowing coals; his slippers lay on the hearth, and his Christmas "easy jacket" hung over the back of his great armchair; his books lay open under the student lamp, and there were two vases of fresh flowers in the room: that was Polly's doing.

"Mrs. Oliver was awake and listening for me, worrying about me, probably; I dare say she thought I'd been waylaid by bandits," he muttered discontentedly. "I might as well live in the Young Women's Christian Association! I can't get mad with an angel, but I didn't intend being one myself! Good gracious! Why don't they hire me a nurse and buy me a perambulator!"

But all the rest was perfect; and his chief chums envied him after they had spent an evening with the Olivers. Polly and he had ceased to quarrel, and were on good, frank, friendly terms. "She is no end of fun," he would have told you; "has no nonsensical young-lady airs about her, is always ready for sport, sings all kinds of songs from grave to gay, knows a good joke when you tell one, and keeps a fellow up to the mark as well as a maiden aunt."

All this was delightful to everybody concerned. Meanwhile the household affairs were as troublesome as they could well be. Mrs. Oliver developed more serious symptoms, and Dr. George asked the San Francisco physician to call to see her twice a week at least.

The San Francisco physician thought "a year at Carlsbad and a year at Nice would be a good thing"; but, failing these, he ordered copious quantities of expensive drugs, and the reserve fund shrank, though the three hundred and twelve dollars was almost intact.

Poor Mrs. Chadwick sent tearful monthly letters, accompanied by checks of fifty to sixty-five dollars. One of the boarders had died; two had gone away; the season was poor; Ah Foy had returned to China; Mr. Greenwood was difficult about his meals; the roof leaked; provisions were dear; Mrs. Holmes in the next street had decided to take boarders; Eastern people were grumbling at the weather, saying it was not at all as reported in the guidebooks; real estate and rents were very low; she hoped to be able to do better next month; and she was Mrs. Oliver's "affectionate Clementine Churchill Chadwick."

Polly had held a consultation with the principal of her school, who had assured her that as she was so well in advance of her class, she could be promoted the next term, if she desired. Accordingly, she left school in order to be more with her mother, and as she studied with Edgar in the evening, she really lost nothing.

Mrs. Howe remitted four dollars from the monthly rent, in consideration of Spanish lessons given to her two oldest children. This experiment proved a success, and Polly next accepted an offer to come three times a week to the house of a certain Mrs. Baer to amuse (instructively) the four little Baer cubs, while the mother Baer wrote a "History of the Dress-Reform Movement in English-Speaking Nations."

For this service Polly was paid ten dollars a month in gold coin, while the amount of spiritual wealth which she amassed could not possibly be estimated in dollars and cents. The ten dollars was very useful, for it procured the services of a kind, strong woman, who came on these three afternoons of Polly's absence, put the entire house in order, did the mending, rubbed Mrs. Oliver's tired back, and brushed her hair until she fell asleep.

So Polly assisted in keeping the wolf from the door, and her sacrifices watered her young heart and kept it tender. "Money may always be a beautiful thing. It is we who make it grimy."

Edgar shared in the business conferences now. He had gone into convulsions of mirth over Polly's system of accounts, and insisted, much against her will, in teaching her bookkeeping, striving to convince her that the cash could be kept in a single box, and the accounts separated in a book.

These lessons were merry occasions, for there was a conspicuous cavity in Polly's brain where the faculty for mathematics should have been.

"Your imbecility is so unusual that it's a positive inspiration," Edgar would say. "It isn't like any ordinary stupidity; there doesn't seem to be any bottom to it, you know; it's abnormal, it's fascinating, Polly!"

Polly glowed under this unstinted praise. "I am glad you like it," she said. "I always like to have a thing first-class of its kind, though I can't pride myself that it compares with your Spanish accent, Edgar; that stands absolutely alone and unapproachable for badness. I don't worry about my mathematical stupidity a bit since I read Dr. Holmes, who says that everybody has an idiotic area in his mind."

There had been very little bookkeeping tonight. It was raining in torrents. Mrs. Oliver was talking with General M—— in the living room, while Edgar and Polly were studying in the dining room.

Polly laid down her book and leaned back in her chair. It had been a hard day, and it was very discouraging that a new year should come to one's door laden with vexations and anxieties, when everybody naturally expected new years to be happy, through January and February at least.

"Edgar," she sighed plaintively, "I find that this is a very difficult world to live in, sometimes."

Edgar looked up from his book, and glanced at her as she lay back with closed eyes in the Chinese lounging chair. She was so pale, so tired, and so very, very pretty just then, her hair falling in bright confusion round her face, her whole figure relaxed with weariness, and her lips quivering a little, as if she would like to cry if she dared.

Polly with dimples playing hide and seek in rosy cheeks, with dazzling eyes, and laughing lips, and saucy tongue, was sufficiently captivating; but Polly with bright drops on her lashes, with a pathetic droop in the corners of her mouth and the suspicion of a tear in her voice—this Polly was irresistible.

"What's the matter, pretty Poll?"

"Nothing specially new. The Baer cubs were naughty as little demons today. One of them had a birthday party yesterday, with four kinds of frosted cake. Mrs. Baer's system of management isn't like mine, and until

I convince the children I mean what I say, they give me the benefit of the doubt. The Baer place is so large that Mrs. Baer never knows where disobedience may occur, and that she may be prepared she keeps one of Mr. Baer's old slippers on the front porch, one in the carriage house, one in the arbor, one in the nursery, and one under the rose hedge at the front gate. She showed me all these haunts, and told me to make myself thoroughly at home. I felt tempted today, but I resisted."

"You are working too hard, Polly. I propose we do something about Mrs. Chadwick. You are bearing all the brunt of other people's faults and blunders."

"But, Edgar, everything is so mixed: Mrs. Chadwick's year of lease isn't over; I suppose she cannot be turned out by main force, and if we should ask her to leave the house it might go unrented for a month or two, and the loss of that money might be as much as the loss of ten or fifteen dollars a month for the rest of the year. I could complain of her to Dr. George, but there again I am in trouble. If he knew that we are in difficulties, he would offer to lend us money in an instant, and that would make mamma ill, I am sure; for we are under all sorts of obligations to him now, for kindnesses that can never be repaid. Then, too, he advised us not to let Mrs. Chadwick have the house. He said that she hadn't energy enough to succeed; but mamma was so sorry for her, and so determined to give her a chance, that she persisted in letting her have it. We shall have to find a cheaper flat, by and by, for I've tried every other method of economizing, for fear of making mamma worse with the commotion of moving."

X

Edgar's Confession

"I'm AFRAID I make it harder, Polly, and you and your mother must be frank with me, and turn me out of the Garden of Eden the first moment I become a nuisance. Will you promise?"

"You are a help to us, Edgar; we told you so the other night. We couldn't have Yung Lee unless you lived with us, and I couldn't earn any money if I had to do all the housework."

"I'd like to be a help, but I'm so helpless!"

"We are all poor together just now, and that makes it easier."

"I am worse than poor!" Edgar declared.

"What can be worse than being poor?" asked Polly, with a sigh drawn from the depths of her boots.

155

"To be in debt," said Edgar, who had not the slight-est intention of making this remark when he opened his lips.

Now the Olivers had only the merest notion of Ed-gar's college troubles; they knew simply what the No-bles had told them, that he was in danger of falling behind his class. This, they judged, was a contingency no longer to be feared; as various remarks dropped by the students who visited the house, and sundry bits of information contributed by Edgar himself, in sudden bursts of high spirits, convinced them that he was re-gaining his old rank, and certainly his old ambition.

"To be in debt," repeated Edgar doggedly, "and to see no possible way out of it. Polly, I'm in a peck of trouble! I've lost money, and I'm at my wits' end to get straight again!"

"Lost money? How much? Do you mean that you lost your pocketbook?"

"No, no; not in that way."

"You mean that you spent it," said Polly. "You mean you overdrew your allowance."

"Of course I did. Good gracious, Polly! There are other ways of losing money than by dropping it in the road. I believe girls don't know anything more about the world than the geography tells them—that it's a round globe like a ball or an orange!"

"Don't be impolite. The less they know about the old world the better they get on, I dare say. Your colossal fund of worldly knowledge doesn't seem to make you very happy, just now. How could you lose your money, I ask? You're nothing but a student, and you are not in any business, are you?"

"I'm in a peck of trouble," Edgar said

"Yes, I am in business, and pretty bad business it is, too."

"What do you mean?"

"I mean that I've been winding myself up into a hard knot, the last six months, and the more I try to disentangle myself, the worse the thing gets. My allowance isn't half enough; nobody but a miser could live on it. I've been unlucky, too. I bought a dog, and someone poisoned him before I could sell him; then I lamed a horse from the livery stable, and had to pay damages; and so it went. The fellows all kept lending me money, rather than let me stay out of the little club suppers, and since I've shut down on expensive gaieties they've gone back on me, and all want their money at once; so does the livery-stable keeper, and the owner of the dog, and a dozen other individuals; in fact, the debtors' prison yawns before me."

"Upon my word, I'm ashamed of you!" said Polly, with considerable heat. "To waste money in that way, when you knew perfectly well you couldn't afford it, was—well, it was downright dishonest, that's what it was! To hear you talk about dogs, and lame horses, and club suppers, anybody would suppose you were a sporting man! What else do they do in that charming college set of yours?"

"I might have known you would take that tone, but I didn't, somehow. I told you just because I thought you were the one girl in a thousand who would understand and advise a fellow when he knows he's made a fool of himself. I didn't suppose you would call me names, and be so unsympathizing, after all we have gone through together!"

"I'm not!—I didn't!—I won't do it again!" said Polly incoherently, as she took a straight chair, planted her elbows on the table, and leaned her chin in her two palms. "Now let's talk about it; tell me everything quickly. How much is it?"

"Nearly two hundred dollars! Don't shudder so provokingly, Polly; that's a mere bagatelle for a college man, but I know it's a good deal for me—a good deal more than I know how to get, at all events."

"Where is the debtors' prison?" asked Polly in an awestruck whisper.

"Oh, there isn't any such thing nowadays! I was only joking; but of course, the men to whom I am in debt can apply to father, and get me in a regular mess. I've pawned my watch to stave one of them off. You see, Polly, I would rather die than do it; nevertheless, I would write and tell father everything, and ask him for the money, but circumstances conspire just at this time to make it impossible. You know he bought that great ranch in Ventura county with Albert Harding of New York. Harding has died insolvent, and father has to make certain payments or lose control of a valuable property. It's going to make him a rich man some time, but for a year or two we shall have to count every penny. Of course the fruit crop this season has been the worst in ten years, and of course there has been a frost this winter, the only severe one within the memory of the oldest inhabitant—that's the way it always is—and there I am! I suppose you despise me, Polly?"

"Yes, I do!" (hotly)—"No, I don't altogether, and I'm not good enough myself to be able to despise people. Besides, you are not a despisable boy. You were born manly and generous and true-hearted, and these hateful things that you have been doing are not a part of your nature a bit; but I'm ashamed of you for yielding to bad impulses when you have so many good ones, and—oh dear!—I do that very same thing myself, now that I stop to think about it. But how could you, *you*, Edgar Noble, take that evil-eyed, fat-nosed, common Tony Selling for a friend? I wonder at you!"

"He isn't so bad in some ways. I owe him eighty dollars of that money, and he says he'll give me six months to pay it."

"I'm glad he has some small virtues," Polly replied witheringly. "Now, what can we do, Edgar? Let us think. What can, what *can* we do?" And she leaned forward reflectively, clasping her knee with her hands and wrinkling her brow with intense thought.

That little "we" fell on Edgar's loneliness of spirit consolingly; for it adds a new pang to self-distrust when righteous people withdraw from one in utter disdain.

"If you can save something each month out of your allowance, Edgar," said Polly, finally, with a brighter look, "I can spare fifty or even seventy-five dollars of our money, and you may pay it back as you can. We are not likely to need it for several months, and your father and mother ought not to be troubled with this matter, now that it's over and done with."

The blood rushed to Edgar's face as he replied stiffly: "I may be selfish and recklessly extravagant, but I don't borrow money from girls. If you wanted to add the last touch to my shame, you've done it. Don't you suppose I have eyes, Polly Oliver? Don't you suppose I've hated myself ever since I came under this roof, when I have seen the way you worked and planned and plotted and saved and denied yourself? Don't you suppose I've looked at you twenty times a day, and said to myself, 'You miserable, selfish puppy, getting yourself and everybody who cares for you into trouble, just look at that girl and be ashamed of yourself down to the ground!' And now you offer to lend me money! Oh, Polly, I wouldn't have believed it of you!"

Polly felt convicted of sin, although she was not very clear as to the reason. She blushed as she said hastily, "Your mother has been a very good friend to us, Edgar; why shouldn't we help you a little, just for once? Now, let us go in to see mamma and talk it all over together!"

"If you pity me, Polly, don't tell her; I could not bear to have that saint upon earth worried over my troubles; it was mean enough to add a feather's weight to yours."

"Well, we won't do it, then," said Polly, with maternal kindness in her tone. "Do stop pacing up and down like a caged panther. We'll find some other way out of the trouble; but boys are such an anxiety! Do you think, Edgar, that you have reformed?"

"Bless your soul! I've kept within my allowance for two or three months. As Susan Nipper says, 'I may be a camel, but I'm not a dromedary!' When I found out where I was, I stopped. I had to stop, and I knew it. I'm all right now, thanks to—several things. In fact, I've acquired a kind of appetite for behaving myself now, and if the rascally debts were only out of the way, I should be the happiest fellow in the universe."

"You cannot apply to your father, so there is only one thing to do—that is, to earn the money."

"But how, when I'm in the classroom three fourths of the day?"

"I don't know," said Polly hopelessly. "I can tell you what to do, but not how to do it."

"I must stay in college, and I must dig and make up for lost time; so most of my evenings will be occupied."

"You must put all your 'musts' together," said Polly decisively, "and then build a bridge over them, or tunnel through them, or span them with an arch. We'll keep thinking about it, and I'm sure something will turn up; I'm not discouraged a bit. You see, Edgar," and Polly's face flushed with feeling as she drew patterns on the tablecloth with her tortoise-shell comb, "you see, of course, the good fairies are not going to leave you in the lurch when you've turned your back on the ugly temptations, and are doing your very best. And now that we've talked it all over, Edgar, I'm not ashamed of you! Mamma and I have been so proud of your successes the last month. She believes in you!"

"Of course," said Edgar dolefully, "because she knows only the best."

"But I know the best and the worst too, and I believe in you! It seems to me the best is always the truest part of one, after all. No, we are not going to be naughty any more; we are going to earn that hateful Tony's money; we are going to take all the class honors, just for fun, not because we care for such trifles, and we are going home for the summer holidays in a blaze of glory!"

Edgar rose with a lighter heart in his breast than he had felt there for many a week. "Good night, Parson Polly," he said rather formally, for he was too greatly touched to be able to command his tones; "add your prayers to your sermons, and perhaps you'll bring the black sheep safely into the fold."

The quick tears rushed to Polly's eyes, for Edgar's stiff manner sat curiously on him, and she feared she had annoyed him by too much advice. "Oh, Edgar," she said, with a quivering lip, "I didn't mean to pose or to preach! You know how full of faults I am, and if I were a boy I should be worse! I was only trying to help a little, even if I am younger and a girl! Don't—don't think I was setting myself up as better than you; that's so mean and conceited and small! Edgar dear, I am so proud to think you told me your troubles; don't turn away from me, or I shall think you are sorry you trusted me!" And Polly laid a persuasive, disarming hand on the lad's shoulder.

Suddenly Edgar's heart throbbed with a new feeling. He saw as in a vision the purity, fidelity, and tender yearning of a true woman's nature shining through a girl's eyes. In that moment he wished as never before to be manly and worthy. He seemed all at once to understand his mother, his sister, all women better, and with a quick impulsive gesture which he would not have understood a month before, he bent his head over astonished Polly's hand, kissed it reverently, then opened the door and went to his room without a word.

XI

The Lady in Black

"I'VE HAD a little adventure," said Polly to her mother one afternoon. "I went out, for the sake of the ride, on the Sutter Street cablecars with Milly Foster. When we came to the end of the line, Milly walked down to Geary Street to take her car home. I went with her to the corner, and as I was coming back I saw a lady in black alighting from an elegant carriage. She had a coachman and a footman, both with weeds on their hats, and she seemed very sad and grave; but she had such a sweet, beautiful face that I was sorry for her the first moment I looked at her. She walked along in front of me toward the cemetery, and there we met those boys that stand about the gate with bouquets. She glanced at the flowers as if she would like to buy some,

but you know how hideous they always are, every color
of the rainbow crowded in tightly together, and she
looked away, dissatisfied. I don't know why she hadn't
brought some with her—she looked rich enough to buy
a whole conservatory; perhaps she hadn't expected to
drive there. However, Milly Foster had given me a
whole armful of beautiful flowers—you know she has a
'white garden.' There were white sweet peas, Lamarque
roses, and three stalks of snowy Eucharist lilies. I didn't
stop to think twice; I just stepped up to her and said,
'I should like to give you my flowers, please. I don't
need them, and I am sure they are just sweet and lovely
enough for the place you want to lay them.'

"The tears came into her eyes—she was just ready
to cry at anything, you know—and she took them at
once, and said, squeezing my hand very tightly, 'I will
take them, dear. The grave of my own, and my only,
little girl lies far away from this—the snow is falling on
it today—but whenever I cannot give the flowers to
her, I always find the resting places of other children,
and lay them there. I know it makes her happy, for she
was born on Christmas Day, and she was full of the
Christmas spirit, always thinking of other people, never
of herself.'

"She did look so pale, and sad, and sweet, that I began to think of you without your troublesome Polly, or
your troublesome Polly without you; and she was
pleased with the flowers and glad that I understood,
and willing to love anything that was a girl or that was
young—oh, you know, mamacita—and so I began to
cry a little, too; and the first thing I knew I kissed her,

which was most informal, if not positively impertinent. But she seemed to like it, for she kissed me back again, and I ran and jumped on the car, and here I am! You will have to eat your dinner without any flowers, madam, for you have a vulgarly strong, healthy daughter, and the poor lady in black hasn't."

This was Polly's first impression of "the lady in black," and thus began an acquaintance which was destined before many months to play a very important part in Polly's fortunes and misfortunes.

What the lady in black thought of Polly, then and subsequently, was told at her own fireside, where she sat, some six weeks later, chatting over an after-dinner cup of coffee with her brother-in-law.

"Take the armchair, John," said Mrs. Bird, "for I have lots to tell you, as the young folks say. I was in the Children's Hospital about five o'clock today. I haven't been there for three months, and I felt guilty about it. The matron asked me to go upstairs into the children's sitting room, the one Donald and I fitted up in memory of Carol. She said that a young lady was telling stories to the children, but that I might go right up and walk in. I opened the door softly, though I don't think the children would have noticed if I had fired a cannon in their midst, and stood there, spellbound by the loveliest, most touching scene I ever witnessed. The room has an open fire, and in a low chair, with the firelight shining on her face, sat that charming, impulsive girl who gave me the flowers at the cemetery—I told you about her. She was telling stories to the children. There were fifteen or twenty of them in the room, all the semi-invalids and convalescents. I should think, and they were gathered about her like flies round a saucer of honey. Every child that could, was doing its best to get a bit of her dress to touch, or a finger of her hand to hold, or an inch of her chair to lean upon. They were the usual pale, weary-looking children, most of them with splints and weights and crutches, and through the folding doors that opened into the next room I could see three more tiny things sitting up in their cots and drinking in every word with eagerness and transport.

"And I don't wonder. There is magic in that girl for sick or sorrowing people. I wish you could have seen and heard her. Her hair is full of warmth and color; her lips and cheeks are pink; her eyes are bright with health and mischief, and beaming with love, too; her smile is like sunshine, and her voice as glad as a wild bird's. I never saw a creature so alive and radiant, and I could feel that the weak little creatures drank in her strength and vigor, without depleting her, as flowers drink in the sunlight.

"As she stood up and made ready to go, she caught sight of me, and exclaimed, with the most astonished face, 'Why, it is my lady in black!' Then, with a blush, she added, 'Excuse me! I spoke without thinking—I always do. I have thought of you very often since I gave you the flowers; and as I didn't know your name, I have always called you my lady in black.'

" 'I should be very glad to be your "lady" in any color,' I answered, 'and my other name is Mrs. Bird.' Then I asked her if she would not come and see me. She said, 'Yes, with pleasure,' and told me also that her mother was ill, and that she left her as little as possible; whereupon I offered to go and see her instead.

"Now, here endeth the first lesson, and here beginneth the second, namely, my new plan, on which I wish to ask your advice. You know that all the money Donald and I used to spend on Carol's nurses, physicians, and what not, we give away each Christmas Day in memory of her. It may be that we give it in monthly installments, but we try to plan it and let people know about it on that day. I propose to create a new profession for talented young women who like to be helpful to others as well as to themselves. I propose to offer this little Miss Oliver, say twenty-five dollars a month, if she will go regularly to the Children's Hospital and to the various orphan asylums just before supper and just before bedtime, and sing and tell stories to the children for an hour. I want to ask her to give two hours a day only, going to each place once or twice a week; but of course she will need a good deal of time for preparation. If she accepts, I will see the managers of the various institutions, offer her services, and arrange for the hours. I am confident that they will receive my protégée with delight, and I am sure that I shall bring the good old art of storytelling into fashion again, through this gifted girl. Now, John, what do you think?"

"I heartily approve, as usual. It is a novelty, but I cannot see why it's not perfectly expedient, and I certainly can think of no other way in which a monthly expenditure of twenty-five dollars will carry so much genuine delight and comfort to so many different chil-

'dren. Carol would sing for joy if she could know of your plan."

"Perhaps she does know it," said Mrs. Bird softly.

And so it was settled.

Polly's joy and gratitude at Mrs. Bird's proposal baffles the powers of the narrator. It was one of those things pleasant to behold, charming to imagine, but impossible to describe. After Mrs. Bird's carriage had been whirled away, she watched at the window for Edgar, and, when she saw him nearing the steps, did not wait for him to unlock the door, but opened it from the top of the stairs, and flew down them to the landing as lightly as a feather.

As for Edgar himself, he was coming up with unprecedented speed, and they nearly fell into each other's arms as they both exclaimed, in one breath, "Hurrah!" and then, in another, "Who told you?"

"How did you know it?" asked Edgar. "Has Tom Mills been here?"

"What is anybody by the name of Mills to me in my present state of mind!" exclaimed Polly. "Have you some good news, too? If so, speak out quickly."

"Good news? I should think I had; what else were you hurrahing about? I've won the scholarship, and I have a chance to earn some money! Tom Mills's eyes are in bad condition, and the oculist says he must wear dark glasses and not look at a book for two months. His father wrote to me today, and he asks if I will read over the day's lessons with Tom every afternoon or evening, so that he can keep up with the class; and says that if I will do him this great service he will be glad to pay me any reasonable sum. He 'ventured' to write me on Professor Hope's recommendation."

"Oh, Edgar, that is too, too good!" cried Polly, jumping up and down in delight. "Now hear my news. What do you suppose has happened?"

"Turned-up noses have come into style."

"Insulting! That isn't the spirit I showed when you told me your good news."

"You've found the leak in the gas stove."

"On the contrary, I don't care if all the gas in our establishment leaks from now to the millennium. Guess again, stupid!"

"Somebody has left you a million."

"No, no!" (scornfully.) "Well, I can't wait your snail's pace. My lady in black, Mrs. Donald Bird, has been here all the afternoon, and she offers me twenty-five dollars a month to give up the Baer cubs and tell stories two hours a day in the orphan asylums and the Children's Hospital! Just what I love to do! Just what I always longed to do! Just what I would do if I were a billionaire! Isn't it heavenly?"

"Well, well! We are in luck, Polly. Hurrah! Fortune smiles at last on the Noble-Oliver household. Let's celebrate! Oh, I forgot. Tom Mills wants to come to dinner. Do you mind?"

"Let him come, goggles and all; we'll have the lame and the halt, as well as the blind, if we happen to see any. Mamma won't care. I told her we'd have a feast tonight that should vie with any of the old Roman banquets! Here's my purse. Please go down on Sutter Street—ride both ways—and buy anything extravagant and unseasonable you can find. Get forced tomatoes; we'll have 'chops and tomato sauce' à la Mrs. Bardell; order fried oysters in a browned loaf; get a quart of ice cream, the most expensive variety they have, a loaf of the richest cake in the bakery, and two chocolate éclairs apiece. Buy hothouse roses, or orchids, for the table, and give five cents to that dirty little boy on the corner there. In short, as Frank Stockton says, 'Let us so live while we are up that we shall forget we have ever been down'!" And Polly plunged upstairs to make a toilet worthy of the occasion.

The banquet was such a festive occasion that Yung Lee's Chinese reserve was sorely tried, and he giggled more than once, while waiting on the table.

Polly had donned a trailing black silk skirt of her mother's, with a white chuddah shawl for a court train, and a white lace blouse to top it. Her hair was wound into a knot on the crown of her head and presented a most magnificent and queenly appearance.

Tom Mills, whose father was four times a millionaire, wondered why they never had such gay times at his home, and tried to fancy his sister Blanche sparkling and glowing and beaming over the prospect of earning twenty-five dollars a month.

Then, when bedtime came, Polly and her mother talked it all over in the dark.

"Oh, mamacita, I am so happy! It's such a lovely beginning, and I shall be so glad, so glad to do it! I hope Mrs. Bird didn't invent the plan for my good, for I have been frightfully shabby each time she has seen me, but she says she thinks of nothing but the children. Now we will have some pretty things, won't we? And oh! do you think, not just now, but some time in the distant centuries, I can have a string of gold beads?"

"I do, indeed," sighed Mrs. Oliver. "You are certainly in no danger of being spoiled by luxury in your youth, my poor little Pollykins; but you will get all these things some time, I feel sure, if they are good for you, and if they belong to you."

XII

The Great Silence

THE MONTHS of April and May were happy ones. The weather was perfect, as only California weather understands the art of being; the hills were at their greenest; the wind almost forgot to blow; the fields blazed in wild flowers; day after day rose in cloudless splendor, and day after day the Golden Gate shone like a sapphire in the sun.

Polly was inwardly nervous. She had the "awe of prosperity" in her heart, and everything seemed too bright to last.

Both she and Edgar were very busy. But work that one loves is no hardship, especially when one is strong and young and hopeful, and when one has great matters at stake, such as the health and wealth of an invalid mother, or the paying off of disagreeable debts.

Even the limp Mrs. Chadwick shared in the general joy; for Mr. Greenwood was so utterly discouraged with her mismanagement of the house, so determined not to fly to ills he knew not of, and so anxious to bring order out of chaos, that on the spur of the moment one day he married her. On the next day he discharged the cook, hired a better one the third, dunned the delinquent boarder the fourth, and collected from him on the fifth; so the May check (signed Clementine Chadwick Greenwood) was made out for eighty-five dollars.

But in the midst of it all, when everything in the outside world danced with life and vigor, and the little house could hardly hold its sweet content—without a glimmer of warning, without a moment's fear or dread, without the precious agony of parting, Mrs. Oliver slipped softly, gently, safely, into the Great Silence.

Mercifully it was Edgar, not Polly, who found her in her accustomed place on the cushions, lying with closed eyelids and smiling lips.

It was half past five. . . . Polly must have gone out at four, as usual, and would be back in half an hour. . . . Yung Lee was humming softly in the little kitchen. . . . In five minutes Edgar Noble had suffered, lived, and grown ten years. He was a man. . . . And then came Polly—and Mrs. Bird with her, thank Heaven!— Polly breathless and glowing, looking up at the bay window for her mother's smile of welcome.

In a few seconds the terrible news was broken, and Polly, overpowered with its awful suddenness, dropped before it as under a physical blow.

It was better so. Mrs. Bird carried her home for the night, as she thought, but a merciful blur stole over the child's tired brain, and she lay for many weeks in a weary illness of delirium and stupor and fever.

Meanwhile, Edgar acted as brother, son, and man of the house. He it was who managed everything, from the first sorrowful days up to the closing of the tiny upper flat where so much had happened: not great things of vast outward importance, but small ones— little miseries and mortifications and struggles and self-denials and victories, that made the past half year a milestone in his life.

A week finished it all! It takes a very short time, he thought, to scatter to the winds of heaven all the gracious elements that make a home. Only a week; and in the first days of June, Edgar went back to Santa Barbara for the summer holidays without even a sight of his brave, helpful girl comrade.

He went back to his brother's congratulations, his sister's kisses, his mother's happy tears, and his father's hearty handclasp, full of renewed pride and belief in his eldest son. But there was a shadow on the lad's high spirits as he thought of gay, courageous, daring Polly, stripped in a moment of all that made life dear.

"I wish we could do something for her, poor little soul," he said to his mother in one of their long talks in the orange-tree sitting room. "I cannot tell what Mrs. Oliver has been to me, and I'm not a bit ashamed to own up to Polly's influence, even if she is two or three years younger than I am. Hang it! I'd like to see the fellow that could live under the same roof as those two women, and not do the best that was in him! Hasn't Polly some relatives in the East?"

"No near ones, and none that she has ever seen. Still, she is not absolutely alone, as many girls would be under like circumstances. We would be only too glad to have her here; the Howards have telegraphed asking her to spend the winter with them in Cambridge; I am confident Dr. Winship will do the same. And Mrs. Bird seems to have constituted herself a sort of Fairy God-mother in chief. You see, everybody loves Polly; and she will probably have no less than four homes open to her. The fact is, if you should put Polly on a desert island, the bees and the butterflies and the birds would gather about her; she draws everything and everybody to her magically. Then, too, she is not penniless. Rents are low, and she cannot hope to get quite as much for the house as before, but even counting repairs, taxes, and furnishings, we think she is reasonably certain of fifty dollars a month."

"She will never be idle, unless this sorrow makes a great change in her. Polly seems to have been created to 'become' by 'doing.' "

Meanwhile Polly, it must be confessed, was not at the present time quite justifying the good opinion of her friends.

She had few of the passive virtues. She could bear sharp stabs of misfortune, which fired her energy and pride, but she resented pin pricks. She could carry heavy, splendid burdens cheerfully, but she fretted under humble cares. She could serve by daring, but not by waiting. She would have gone to the stake or the scaffold, I think, with tolerable grace; but she would probably have recanted any article of faith if she had been confronted with life imprisonment.

Trouble that she took upon herself for the sake of others, and out of love, she accepted sweetly. Sorrows that she did not choose, which were laid upon her without her consent, and which were "just the ones she did *not* want, and did *not* need, and would *not* have, and could *not* bear"—these sorrows found her unwilling, bitter, and impatient.

Yet if life is a school and we all have lessons to learn in it, the Great Teacher will be unlikely to set us tasks which we have already finished. Some review there must be, for certain things are specially hard to keep in mind, and have to be gone over and over, lest they fade into forgetfulness. But there must be continued progress in a life school. There is no parrot repetition, sing-song, meaningless, of words that have ceased to be vital. New lessons are to be learned as fast as the old ones are understood. Of what use to set Polly tasks to develop her bravery, when she was already brave?

Courage was one of the little jewels set in her fairy crown when she was born, but there was a round, empty space beside it, where Patience should have been. Further along was Daring, making a brilliant show, but again there was a tiny vacancy waiting for Prudence.

The crown made a fine appearance, on the whole, because the large jewels were mostly in place, and the light of these blinded you to the lack of the others; but to the eye of the keen observer there was a want of symmetry and completeness.

Polly knew the unfinished state of her fairy crown as well as anybody else. She could not plead ignorance as an excuse; but though she would have gone on polishing the great gems with a fiery zeal, she added the little jewels very slowly, and that only on compulsion.

There had been seven or eight weeks of partial unconsciousness, when the sorrow and the loneliness of life stole into her waking dreams only vaguely and at intervals; when she was unhappy, and could not remember why; and slept, to wake and wonder and sleep again.

Then there were days and weeks when the labor of living was all that the jaded body could accomplish; when memory was weak; when life began at the pillow, and ended at the foot of the bed, and the universe was bounded by the bedroom windows.

But when her strength came back, and she stood in the middle of the floor, clothed and in her right mind, well enough to remember—oh! then indeed the deep waters of bitterness rolled over poor Polly's head and into her heart, and she sank beneath them without a wish or a struggle to rise.

"If it had been anything else!" she sobbed. "Why did God take away my most precious, my only one to live for, when I was trying to take care of her, trying to be good, trying to give back the strength that had been poured out on me—miserable, worthless me! Surely, if a girl was willing to do without a father and sisters and brothers, without good times and riches, willing to work like a galley slave, willing to scrimp and plan and save for ever and ever; surely 'they' might be willing that she should keep her mother!"

Poor Polly! Providence at this time seemed nothing more than a collection of demons which she classified under the word "they," and which she felt certain were scourging her pitilessly and needlessly. She could not see any reason or justification in "their" cruelties—for that was the only term she could apply to her afflictions.

Mrs. Bird had known sorrow, and she did her best to minister to the troubled little heart; but it was so torn that it could be healed only by the soft balm of Time.

Perhaps, a long while after such a grief—it is always "perhaps" in a great crisis, though the certainty is ours if we will but grasp it—perhaps the hidden meaning of the sorrow steals gently into our softened hearts. We see, as in a vision, a new light by which to work; we rise, cast off the outgrown shell, and build us a more stately mansion, in which to dwell till God makes that home also too small to hold the evergrowing soul!

XIII

The Banyan Tree

———

In August Mr. John Bird took Polly to the Nobles'
ranch in Santa Barbara, in the hope that the old scenes
and old friends might soothe her, and give her strength
to take up the burden of life with something of her
former sunshiny spirit.

Edgar was a junior now, back at his work, sunburned
and strong from his summer's outing. He had seen
Polly twice after his return to San Francisco; but the
first meeting was an utter failure, and the second nearly
as trying. Neither of them could speak of the subject
that absorbed their thoughts, nor had either courage
enough to begin other topics of conversation. The mere
sight of Edgar was painful to the girl now, it brought to
mind so much that was dear, so much that was past and
gone.

In the serenity of the ranch life, the long drives with Margery and Philip, the quiet chats with Mrs. Noble, Polly gained somewhat in strength; but the old spring, vitality, and enthusiasm had vanished for the time, and the little circle of friends marveled at this Polly without her nonsense, her ready smiles, her dancing dimples, her extravagances of speech.

Once a week, at least, Dr. George would steal an hour or two, and saddle his horse to take Polly for a gallop over the hills, through the canyons, or on the beach.

His half-grave, half-cheery talks on these rides did her much good. He sympathized and understood and helped, even when he chided, and Polly sometimes forgot her own troubles in wondering whether Dr. George had not suffered and overcome a good many of his own.

"You make one great error, my child," he once said, in response to one of Polly's outbursts of grief, "and it is an error young people very naturally fall into. You think that no one was ever chastened as you are. You say, with Jeremiah, 'No prophet is afflicted like unto this prophet!' Now you are simply bearing your own share of the world's trouble. How can you hope to escape the universal lot? There are dozens of people within sight of this height of land who have borne as much, and must bear as much again. I know this must seem a hard philosophy, and I should not preach it to any but a stout little spirit like yours, my Polly. These things come to all of us; they are stern facts; they are here, and they must be borne; but it makes all the difference in the world how we bear them. We can clench our fists, close our lips tightly, and say, 'Since I must, I can'; or we can look up and say cheerfully, 'I will!' The first method is philosophical and strong enough, but there is no sweetness in it. If you have this burden to carry, make it as light, not as heavy, as you can; if you have this grief to endure, you want at least to come out of it sweeter and stronger than ever before. It seems a pity to let it go for nothing. In the largest sense of the word, you can live for your mother now as truly as you did in the old times; you know very well how she would have had you live."

Polly felt a sense of shame steal over her as she looked at Dr. George's sweet, strong smile and resolute mouth, and she said, with the hint of a new note in her voice:

"I see, and I will try; but how does one ever learn to live without loving—I mean the kind of loving I had in my life? I know I can live for my mother in the largest sense of the word, but to me all the comfort and sweetness seems to tuck itself under the word in its 'little' sense. I shall have to go on developing and developing until I am almost developed to death, and go on growing and growing in grace until I am ready to be caught up in a chariot of fire, before I can love my mother 'in the largest sense of the word.' I want to cuddle my head on her shoulder, that's what I want. Oh, Dr. George, how does one contrive to be good when one is not happy? How can one walk in the right path when there doesn't seem to be any brightness to go by?"

"My dear little girl," and Dr. George looked soberly

out on the ocean, dull and lifeless under the gray October sky, "when the sun of one's happiness is set, one lights a candle called 'Patience,' and guides one's footsteps by that!"

"If only I were not a rich heiress," said Polly next morning, "I dare say I should be better off; for then I simply couldn't have gone to bed for two or three months, and idled about like this for another. But there seems to be no end to my money. Edgar paid all the bills in San Francisco, and saved twenty out of our precious three hundred and twelve dollars. Then Mrs. Greenwood's rent money has been accumulating four months, while I have been visiting you and Mrs. Bird; and the Greenwoods are willing to pay sixty dollars a month for the house still, even though times are dull; so I am hopelessly wealthy—but on the whole I am very glad. The old desire to do something, and be something, seems to have faded out of my life with all the other beautiful things. I think I shall go to a girls' college and study, or find some other way of getting through the hateful, endless years that stretch out ahead! Why, I am only a little past seventeen, and I may live to be ninety! I do not see how I can ever stand this sort of thing for seventy-three years!"

Mrs. Noble smiled in spite of herself. "Just apply yourself to getting through this year, Polly dear, and let the other seventy-two take care of themselves. They will bring their own cares and joys and responsibilities and problems, little as you realize it now. This year, grievous as it seems, will fade by and by, until you can look back at it with resignation and without tears."

"I don't want it to fade!" cried Polly passionately. "I never want to look back at it without tears! I want to be faithful always; I want never to forget, and never to feel less sorrow than I do this minute!"

"Take that blue-covered Emerson on the table, Polly; open it at the essay on 'Compensation,' and read the page marked with the orange leaf."

The tears were streaming down Polly's cheeks, but she opened the book, and read with a faltering voice:

"We cannot part with our f-fr-friends. We cannot let our angels go. [Sob.] We do not see that they only go out that archangels may come in. . . . We do not believe there is any force in today to rival or recreate that beautiful yesterday. [Sob.] We linger in the ruins of the old tent where once we had shelter. . . . We cannot

again find aught so dear, so sweet, so graceful. [Sob.]
But we sit and weep in vain. We cannot stay amid the
ruins. The voice of the Almighty saith, 'Up and onward
for evermore!' . . . The sure years reveal the deep
remedial force that underlies all sorrow. . . . The man
or woman who would have remained a sunny garden
flower, with no room for its roots and too much sunshine for its head, by the falling of the walls and the
neglect of the gardener is made the banyan of the
forest, yielding shade and fruit to wide neighborhoods
of men."

"Do you see, Polly?"

"Yes, I see; but oh, I was so happy being a garden
flower with the sunshine on my head, and I can't seem
to care the least little bit for being a banyan tree!"

"Well," said Mrs. Noble, smiling through her own
tears, "I fear that God will never insist on your 'yielding shade and fruit to wide neighborhoods of men' unless you desire it. Not all sunny garden flowers become
banyan trees by the falling of the walls. Some of them
are crushed beneath the ruins, and never send any
more color or fragrance into the world."

"The garden flower had happiness before the walls
fell," said Polly. "It is happiness I want."

"The banyan tree had blessedness after the walls fell,
and it is blessedness I want; but then, I am forty-seven,
and you are seventeen!" sighed Mrs. Noble, as they
walked through the orange orchard to the house.

XIV

Scarlet Runners

———————

ONE DAY, in the middle of October, the mail brought Polly two letters: the first from Edgar, who often dashed off cheery scrawls in the hope of getting cheery replies, which never came; and the second from Mrs. Bird, who had a plan to propose.

Edgar wrote:

. . . "I have a new boarding place in San Francisco, a stone's throw from Mrs. Bird's, whose mansion I can look down upon from a lofty height reached by a flight of fifty wooden steps—good training in athletics! Mrs. Morton is a kind landlady and the house is a home, in a certain way,

> *"But oh, the difference to me*
> *'Twixt tweedledum and tweedledee!*

"There is a Morton girl, too; but she neither plays nor sings nor jokes, nor even looks—in fine, she is not Polly! I have come to the conclusion, now, that girls in a house are almost always nuisances—I mean, of course, when they are not Pollies. Oh, why are you so young, and so loaded with this world's goods, that you will never need me for a boarder again? Mrs. Bird is hoping to see you soon, and I chose my humble lodging on this hilltop because, from my attic's lonely height, I can watch you going in and out of your 'marble halls'; and you will almost pass my door as you take the car. In view of this pleasing prospect (now, alas! somewhat distant), I send you a scrap of newspaper verse which prophesies my sentiments. It is signed 'M. E. W.,' and Tom Mills says whoever wrote it knows you.

WHEN POLLY GOES BY

'T is but poorly I'm lodged in a little side street,
Which is seldom disturbed by the hurry of feet,
For the flood tide of life long ago ebbed away
From its homely old houses, rain-beaten and gray;
And I sit with my pipe in the window, and sigh
At the buffets of fortune—till Polly goes by.

There's a flaunting of ribbons, a flurry of lace,
And a rose in the bonnet above a bright face,
A glance from two eyes so deliciously blue
The midsummer seas scarcely rival their hue;
And once in a while, if the wind's blowing high,
The sound of soft laughter as Polly goes by.

Then up jumps my heart and begins to beat fast.
"She's coming!" it whispers. "She's here! She has passed!"
While I throw up the sash and lean breathlessly down
To catch the last glimpse of her vanishing gown,
Excited, delighted, yet wondering why
My senses desert me if Polly goes by.

Ah! she must be a witch, and the magical spell
She has woven about me has done its work well,
For the morning grows brighter, and gayer the air
That my landlady sings as she sweeps down the stair;
And my poor lonely garret, up close to the sky,
Seems something like heaven when Polly goes by.

"P.S. Tony has returned to the university. He asked after the health of the 'sunset-haired goddess' yesterday. You'd better hurry back and take care of me! No, joking aside, don't worry about me, little missionary; I've outgrown Tony, and I hope I don't need to be reformed oftener than once a year.

"Yours ever,

Edgar.

"P.S. No. II. I saw you twice after—you know—and I was dumb on both occasions. Of all people in the world I ought to have been able to say something helpful to you in your trouble, I, who lived with you and your dear mother through all those happy months before she left us. It will be just the same when I see you again: I shall never be able to speak, partly, I suppose, because I am a man, or on the road to becoming one. I know this is making you cry; I can see the tears in your eyes across all the distance; but it is better even that you should cry than that you should think me cold

or unmindful of your sorrow. Do you know one of the
sacred memories of my life? It is that, on that blessed
night when your mother asked me to come and live under her roof, she said she should be glad to feel that in
any sudden emergency you and she would have a near
friend to lean upon. There was a 'royal accolade,' if you
like! I felt in an instant as if she had bestowed the order of knighthood upon me, and as if I must live more
worthily in order to deserve her trust. How true it is,
Polly, that those who believe in us educate us!

"Do you remember (don't cry, dear!) that night by
the fireside—the night when we brought her out of her
bedroom after three days of illness—when we sat on
either side of her, each holding a hand while she told
us the pretty romance of her meeting and loving your
father? I slipped the loose wedding ring up and down
her finger, and stole a look at her now and then. She
was like a girl when she told that story, and I could not
help thinking it was worth while to be a tender, honorable, faithful man, to bring that look into a woman's
face after eighteen years. Well, I adored her, that is all
I can say; and I can't *say* even that, I have to write it.
Don't rob me, Polly, of the right she gave me, that of
being a 'near friend to lean upon.' I am only afraid,
because you, more than anyone else, know certain weak-
nesses and follies of mine, and, indeed, pulled me out
of the pit and held me up till I got a new footing. I am
afraid you will never have the same respect for me, nor
believe that a fellow so weak as I *was* could be strong
enough to lean upon. Try me once, Polly, just to humor
me, won't you? Give me something to do—something

hard! Lean just a little, Polly, and see how stiff I'll be—
no, bother it, I won't be stiff, I'll be firm! To tell the
truth, I can never imagine you as 'leaning'; though they
say you are pale and sad, and out of sorts with life. You
remind me of one of the gay scarlet runners that climb
up the slender poles in the garden below my window.
The pole holds up the vine at first, of course, but the
vine keeps the pole straight; not in any ugly and com-
monplace fashion, but by winding round and round
about it, and hanging its blossoms in and out and here
and there, till the poor, serviceable pole is forgotten in
the beauty that makes use of it.

"Good-by, little scarlet runner! You will bloom again
some day, when the storm that has beaten you down
has passed over and the sky is clear and the sun warm.
Don't laugh at me, Polly!

"Always yours, whether you laugh or not,

"EDGAR.

"P.S. No. III. I shouldn't dare add this third post-
script if you were near enough to slay me with the
lightning of your eye, but I simply wish to mention that
a wise gardener chooses young, strong timber for *poles,*
—saplings, in fact! *Mr. John Bird is too old for this
purpose.* Well seasoned he is, of course, and suitable as
a prop for a century plant, but not for a scarlet runner!
I like him, you know, but I'm sure he'd crack if you
leaned on him; in point of fact, he's a little cracked
now!

E. N."

The ghost of a smile shone on Polly's April face as
she folded Edgar's letter and laid it in its envelope; first

came a smile, then a tear, then a dimple, then a sob, then a wave of bright color.

"Edgar is growing up so fast," she thought, "I shall soon be afraid to scold him or advise him, and

'What will poor Robin do then, poor thing?'

Upon my word, if I caught him misbehaving nowadays, I believe I should hesitate to remonstrate with him. He will soon be capable of remonstrating with me, at this rate. He is a goose—oh, there's no shadow of doubt as to that, but he's an awfully nice goose."

Mrs. Bird's letter ran thus:

"MY DEAREST POLLYKINS:—We have lived without you just about as long as we can endure it. The boys have returned to school and college. Mr. Bird contemplates one more trip to Honolulu, and brother John and I need someone to coddle and worry over. I have not spoken to you of your future, because I wished to wait until you opened the subject. It is too late for you to begin your professional training this year, and I think you are far too delicate just now to undertake so arduous a work; however, you are young, and that can wait for a bit. As to the storytelling in the hospitals and asylums, I wish you could find courage and strength to go on with that, not for your own sake alone, but for the sake of others.

"As I have told you before, the money is set aside for that special purpose, and the work will be carried on by somebody. Of course I can get a substitute if you refuse, and that substitute may, after a little time, satisfy the impatient children, who flatten their noses against the windowpanes and long for Miss Pauline every day of their meager lives. But I fear the substitute will never be Polly! She may 'rattle round in your place' (as somebody said under different circumstances), but she can never fill it! Why not spend the winter with us, and do this lovely work, keeping up other studies if you are strong enough? It will be so sweet for you to feel that out of your own sadness you can comfort and brighten the lives of these lonely, suffering children and these motherless or fatherless ones. It will seem hard to begin, no doubt; but new life will flow in your veins when you take up your active, useful work again. The joyousness that God put into your soul before you were born, my Polly, is a sacred trust. You must not hide it in a napkin, dear, or bury it, or lose it. It was given to you only that you should share it with others. It was intended for the world at large, though it was bestowed upon you in particular. Come, dear, to one who knows all about it—one whom you are sweet enough to call

"Your Fairy Godmother."

"Mrs. Noble," said Polly, with a sober smile, "the 'Ancon' sails on the 20th, and I am going to sail with her."

"So soon? What for, dear?"

"I am going to be a banyan tree, if you please," answered Polly.

XV

Life in the Birds' Nest

———

POLLY settled down in the Birds' Nest under the protecting wing of Mrs. Bird, and a very soft and unaccustomed sort of shelter it was.

A room had been refurnished expressly for the welcome guest, and as Mrs. Bird pushed her gently in alone, the night of her arrival, she said, "This is the Pilgrim Chamber, Polly. It will speak our wishes for us."

It was not the room in which Polly had been ill for so many weeks; for Mrs. Bird knew the power of associations, and was unwilling to leave any reminder of those painful days to sadden the girl's new life.

As Polly looked about her, she was almost awed by the dazzling whiteness. The room was white enough for an angel, she thought. The straw matting was almost concealed by a mammoth rug made of white Japanese goatskins sewed together; the paint was like snow, and the furniture had all been painted white, save for the delicate silver lines that relieved it. There were soft, full curtains of white muslin fringed with something that looked like thistledown, and the bedstead had an overhanging canopy of the same. An open fire burned in the little grate, and a big white and silver rattan chair was drawn cozily before it. There was a girlish dressing table with its oval mirror draped in dotted muslin; a dainty writing desk with everything convenient upon it; and in one corner was a low bookcase of white satinwood. On the top of this case lay a card, "With the best wishes of John Bird," and along the front of the upper shelf were painted the words: "Come, tell us a story!" Below this there was a rich array of good things. The Grimms, Laboulaye, and Hans Christian Andersen were all there. Mrs. Ewing's "Jackanapes" and Charles Kingsley's "Water Babies" jostled the "Seven Little Sisters" series; Hawthorne's "Wonder Book" lay close to Lamb's "Tales from Shakespeare"; and Whittier's "Child Life in Prose and Poetry" stood between Mary Howitt's "Children's Year" and Robert Louis Stevenson's "Child's Garden of Verses."

Polly sat upon the floor before the bookcase and gloated over her new treasures, each of which bore her name on the fly-leaf.

As her eye rose to the vase of snowy pampas plumes and the pictured Madonna and Child above the bookcase, it wandered still higher until it met a silver motto painted on a blue frieze that finished the top of the walls where they met the ceiling.

Polly walked slowly round the room, studying the il-

Polly sat upon the floor before the bookcase

luminated letters: *"And they laid the Pilgrim in an upper chamber, and the name of the chamber was Peace."*

This brought the ready tears to Polly's eyes. "God seems to give me everything but what I want most," she thought, "but since He gives me so much, I must not question any more; I must not choose; I must believe that He wants me to be happy, after all, and I must begin and try to be good again."

She did try to be good. She came down to breakfast the next morning, announcing to Mrs. Bird, with her grateful morning kiss, that she meant to "live up to" her room. "But it's going to be difficult," she confessed. "I shall not dare to have a naughty thought in it; it seems as if it would be written somewhere on the whiteness!"

"You can come and be naughty in my bachelor den, Polly," said Mr. Bird, smiling. "Mrs. Bird doesn't waste any girlish frills and poetic decorations and mystical friezes on her poor brother-in-law! He is done up in muddy browns, as befits his age and sex."

Polly insisted on beginning her work the very next afternoon; but she had strength only for three appointments a week, and Mrs. Bird looked doubtfully after her as she walked away from the house with a languid gait utterly unlike her old buoyant step.

Edgar often came in the evenings, as did Tom and Blanche Mills, and Milly Foster; but though Polly was cheerful and composed, she seldom broke into her old flights of nonsense.

On other nights, when they were alone, she prepared for her hours of storytelling, and in this she was wonderfully helped by Mr. Bird's suggestions and advice; for he was a student of literature in many languages, and delighted in bringing his treasures before so teachable a pupil.

"She has a sort of genius that astonishes me," said he one morning, as he chatted with Mrs. Bird over the breakfast table.

Polly had excused herself, and stood at the farther library window, gazing up the street vaguely and absently, as if she saw something beyond the hills and the bay. Mrs. Bird's heart sank a little as she looked at the slender figure in the black dress. There were no dimples about the sad mouth, and was it the dress, or was she not very white these latter days?—so white that her hair encircled her face with absolute glory, and startled one with its color.

"It is a curious kind of gift," continued Mr. Bird, glancing at his morning papers. "She takes a long tale of Hans Andersen's, for instance, and after an hour or two, when she has his idea fully in mind, she shows me how she proposes to tell it to the younger children at the orphan asylum. She clasps her hands over her knees, bends forward toward the firelight, and tells the story with such simplicity and earnestness that I am always glad she is looking the other way and cannot see the tears in my eyes. I cried like a schoolgirl last night over 'The Ugly Duckling.' She has natural dramatic instinct, a great deal of facial expression, power of imitation, and an almost unerring taste in the choice of words, which is unusual in a girl so young and one who has been so imperfectly trained. I give her an old legend or some fragment of folklore, and straightway she dishes it up for me as if it had been bone of her bone and marrow of her marrow; she knows just what to leave out and what to put in, somehow. You had one of your happy inspirations about that girl, Margaret—she is a born storyteller. She ought to wander about the country with a lute under her arm. Is the Olivers' house insured?"

"Good gracious, Jack! You have a kangaroo sort of mind! How did you leap to that subject? I'm sure I don't know, but what difference does it make, anyway?"

"A good deal of difference," he answered nervously, looking into the library (yes, Polly had gone out); "because the house, the furniture, and the stable were burned to the ground last night—so the morning paper says."

Mrs. Bird rose and closed the doors. "That does seem too dreadful to be true," she said. "The poor child's one bit of property, her only stand-by in case of need! Oh, it can't be burned; and, if it is, it *must* be insured. I'm afraid a second blow would break her down completely just now, when she has not recovered from the first."

Mr. Bird went out and telegraphed to Dr. George Edgerton:

Is Oliver house burned? What was the amount of insurance, if any? Answer.

JOHN BIRD.

At four o'clock the reply came:

House and outbuildings burned. No insurance. Have written particulars. Nothing but piano and family portraits saved.

GEORGE EDGERTON.

In an hour another message, marked "Collect," followed the first one:

House burned last night. Defective flue. No carelessness on part of servants or family. Piano, portraits, icecream freezer, and washboiler saved by superhuman efforts of husband. Have you any instructions? Have taken to my bed. Accept love and sympathy.

CLEMENTINE CHADWICK GREENWOOD.

So it was true. The buildings were burned, and there was no insurance.

I know you will say there never is, in stories where the heroine's courage is to be tested, even if the narrator has to burn down the whole township to do it satisfactorily. But to this objection I can make only this answer: First, that this house really did burn down; secondly, that there really was no insurance; and thirdly, if this combination of circumstances did not sometimes happen in real life, it would never occur to a storyteller to introduce it as a test for heroes and heroines.

"Well," said Mrs. Bird despairingly, "Polly must be told. Now, will you do it, or shall I? Of course you want me to do it! Men never have any courage about these things, nor any tact either."

At this moment the subject of conversation walked into the room, hat and coat on, and an unwonted color in her cheeks. Edgar Noble followed behind. Polly removed her hat and coat leisurely, sat down on a hassock on the hearth rug, and ruffled her hair with the old familiar gesture, almost forgotten these latter days.

Mrs. Bird looked warningly at the telltale yellow telegrams in Mr. Bird's lap, and strove to catch his eye and indicate to his dull masculine intelligence the necessity of hiding them until they could devise a plan of breaking the sad news.

Mrs. Bird's glance and Mr. Bird's entire obliviousness were too much for Polly's gravity. To their astonishment she burst into a peal of laughter.

> *" 'My lodging is on the cold, cold ground,*
> *And hard, very hard is my fare!' "*

she sang, to the tune of "Believe me, if all those endearing young charms." "So you know all about it, too?"

"How did you hear it?" gasped Mrs. Bird.

"I bought the evening paper to see if that lost child at the asylum had been found. Edgar jumped on the car, and seemed determined that I should not read the paper until I reached home. He was very kind, but slightly bungling in his attentions. I knew then that something was wrong, but just what was beyond my imagination, unless Jack Howard had been expelled from Harvard, or Bell Winship had been lost at sea on the way home; so I persisted in reading, and at last I found the fatal item. I don't know whether Edgar expected me to faint at sight! I'm not one of the fainting sort!"

"I'm relieved that you can take it so calmly. I have been shivering with dread all day, and Jack and I have been quarreling as to which should break it to you."

"Break it to me!" echoed Polly, in superb disdain. "My dear Fairy Godmother, you must think me a weak sort of person! As if the burning down of one patrimonial estate could shatter my nerves! What is a passing home or so? Let it burn, by all means, if it likes. 'He that is down need fear no fall.'"

"It is your only property," said Mr. Bird, trying to present the other side of the case properly, "and it was not insured."

"What of that?" she asked briskly. "Am I not housed and fed like a princess at the present moment? Have I not two hundred and fifty dollars in the bank, and am I not earning twenty-five dollars a month with absolute regularity? Avaunt, cold Fear!"

"How was it that the house was not insured?" asked Mr. Bird.

"I'm sure I don't know. It was insured once upon a time, if I remember right; when it got uninsured, I can't tell. How do things get uninsured, Mr. Bird?"

"The insurance lapses, of course, if the premium isn't regularly paid."

"Oh, that would account for it!" said Polly easily. "There were quantities of things that weren't paid regularly, though they were always paid in course of time. You ought to have asked me if we were insured, Edgar —you were the boy of the house—insurance isn't a girl's department. Let me see the telegrams, please."

They all laughed heartily over Mrs. Greenwood's characteristic message.

"Think of 'husband' bearing that aged ice-cream freezer and that leaky boiler to a place of safety!" exclaimed Polly. " 'All that was left of them, left of six hundred!' Well, my family portraits, piano, freezer, and boiler will furnish a humble cot very nicely in my future spinster days. By the way, the land didn't burn up, I suppose, and that must be good for something, isn't it?"

"Rather," answered Edgar, "a corner lot on the best street in town, four blocks from the new hotel site! It's worth eighteen hundred or two thousand dollars, at least."

"Then why do you worry about me, good people? I'm not a heroine. If I were sitting on the curbstone without a roof to my head, and didn't know where I should get my dinner, I should cry! But I smell my dinner" (here she sniffed pleasurably), "and I think it's chicken! You see, it's so difficult for me to realize that I'm a pauper, living here, a pampered darling in the halls of wealth, with such a large income rolling up daily that I shall be a prey to fortune hunters by the time I am twenty! Pshaw! don't worry about me! This is just the sort of diet I have been accustomed to from my infancy! I rather enjoy it!"

Whereupon Edgar recited an impromptu nonsense verse:

"There's a queer little maiden named Polly,
Who always knows when to be jolly.
    When ruined by fire
    Her spirits rise higher,
This most inconsistent Miss Polly."

XVI

The Candle Called Patience

THE BURNING of the house completely prostrated Mrs. Clementine Churchill Chadwick Greenwood, who, it is true, had the actual shock of the conflagration to upset her nervous system, though she suffered no financial loss.

Mr. Greenwood was heard to remark that he wished he could have foreseen that the house would burn down, for now he should have to move anyway, and if he had known that a few months before, why—

Here the sentence always ended mysteriously, and the neighbors finished it as they liked.

The calamity affected Polly, on the other hand, very much like a tonic. She felt the necessity of "bracing" to meet the fresh responsibilities that seemed waiting for

203

her in the near future; and night and day, in sleeping and waking, resting and working, a plan was formulating itself in the brain just roused from its six months' apathy—a novel, astonishing, enchanting, revolutionary plan, which she bided her time to disclose.

The opportunity came one evening after dinner, when Mrs. Bird and her brother, Edgar and herself, were gathered in the library.

The library was a good place in which to disclose plans, or ask advice, or whisper confidences. The great carved oak mantel held on the broad space above the blazing logs the graven motto, "Esse Quod Opto." The walls were lined with books from floor halfway to ceiling, and from the tops of the cases Plato, Socrates, Marcus Aurelius, and the Sage of Concord looked down with benignant wisdom. The table in the center was covered with a methodical litter of pamphlets and magazines, and a soft light came from the fire and from two tall, shaded lamps.

Mr. Bird, as was his wont, leaned back in his leather chair, puffing delicate rings of smoke into the air. Edgar sat by the center table, idly playing with a paper knife. Mrs. Bird sat in her low rocking chair with a bit of fancywork, and Polly, on the hearthrug, leaned cozily back against her Fairy Godmother's knees.

The clinging tendrils in Polly's nature, left hanging so helplessly when her mother was torn away, reached out more and more to wind themselves about lovely Mrs. Bird, who, notwithstanding her three manly sons, had a place in her heart left sadly vacant by the loss of her only daughter.

Polly broke one of the pleasant silences.

An open fire makes such delightful silences, if you ever noticed. When you sit in a room without it, the gaps in the conversation make everybody seem dull; the last comer rises with embarrassment and thinks he must be going, and you wish that someone would say the next thing and keep the ball rolling. The open fire arranges all these little matters with a perfect tact and grace all its own. It is acknowledged to be the center of attraction, and the people gathered about it are only supernumeraries. It blazes and crackles and snaps cheerily, the logs break and fall, the coals glow and fade and glow again, and the dull man can always poke the fire if his wit desert him. Who ever feels like telling a precious secret over a steam heater?

Polly looked away from everybody and gazed straight into the blaze.

"I have been thinking over a plan for my future work," she said, "and I want to tell it to you and see if you all approve and think me equal to it. It used to come to me in flashes, after this Fairy Godmother of mine opened an avenue for my surplus energy by sending me out as a storyteller; but lately I haven't had any heart for it. Work grew monotonous and disagreeable and hopeless, and I'm afraid I had no wish to be useful or helpful to myself or to anybody else. But now everything is different. I am not so rich as I was (I wish, Mr. Bird, you would not smile so provokingly when I mention my riches!), and I must not be idle any longer; so this is my plan. I want to be a storyteller by profession. Perhaps you will say that nobody has ever done it; but surely that is an advantage; I should have the field to myself for a while, at least. I have dear Mrs. Bird's little poor children as a foundation. Now, I would like to get groups of other children together in somebody's parlor twice a week and tell them stories—the older children one day in the week and the younger ones another. Of course I haven't thought out all the details, because I hoped my Fairy Godmother would help me there, if she approved of my plan; but I have ever so many afternoons all arranged, and enough stories and songs at my tongue's end for three months. Do you think it impossible or nonsensical, Mr. Bird?"

"No," said he thoughtfully, after a moment's pause. "It seems on the first hearing to be perfectly feasible. In fact, in one sense it will not be an experiment at all. You have tried your powers, gained self-possession and command of your natural resources; developed your ingenuity, learned the technicalities of your art, so to speak, already. You propose now, as I understand, to extend your usefulness, widen your sphere of action, address yourself to a larger public, and make a profession out of what was before only a side issue in your life. It's a new field, and it's a noble one, taken in its highest aspect, as you have always taken it. My motto for you, Polly, is Goethe's couplet:

> *'What you can do, or dream you can, begin it.*
> *Boldness has genius, power, and magic in it.'* "

"Make way for the storyteller!" cried Edgar. "I will buy season tickets for both your groups, if you will only make your limit of age include me. I am only five feet ten, and I'll sit very low if you'll admit me to the charmed circle. Shall you have a stage name? I would suggest 'The Seraphic Sapphira.' "

"Now, don't tease," said Polly with dignity, "this is in sober earnest. What do you think, Fairy Godmother? I've written to my dear Miss Mary Denison in Santa Barbara, and she likes the idea."

"I think it is charming. In fact, I can hardly wait to begin. I will be your business manager, my Pollykins, and we'll make it a success, if it is possible. If you'll take me into your confidence and tell me what you mean to do, I will plan the hows and whens and wheres."

"You see, dear people," continued Polly, "it is really the only thing that I know how to do; and I have had several months' experience, so that I'm not entirely untrained. I'm not afraid any more, so long as it is only children; though the presence of one grown person makes me tongue-tied. Grown-up people never know how to listen, somehow, and they make you more conscious of yourself. But when the children gaze up at you with their shining eyes and their parted lips—the smiles just longing to be smiled and the teardrops just waiting to glisten—I don't know what there is about it, but it makes you wish you could go on forever and never break the spell. And it makes you tremble, too, for fear you should say anything wrong. You seem so close to children when you are telling them stories; just as if a little, little silken thread spun itself out from one side of your heart through each of theirs, until it came back to be fastened in your own again; and it holds so tight, so tight, when you have done your best and the children are pleased and grateful."

For days after this discussion Polly felt as if she were dwelling on a mysterious height from which she could see all the kingdoms of the earth. She said little and thought much (oh, that this should come to be written of Polly Oliver!). The past which she had regretted with such passionate fervor still fought for a place among present plans and future hopes. But she was almost convinced in these days that a benevolent Power might after all be helping her to work out her own salvation in an appointed way, with occasional weariness and tears, like the rest of the world.

It was in such a softened mood that she sat alone in church one Sunday afternoon at vespers. She had chosen a place where she was sure of sitting quietly by herself, and where the rumble of the organ and the words of the service would come to her soothingly. The late afternoon sun shone through the stained-glass windows, bringing out the tender blue on the Madonna's gown, the white on the wings of angels and robes of newborn innocents, the glow of rose and carmine, with here and there a glorious gleam of Tyrian purple. Then her eyes fell on a memorial window opposite her. A mother bowed with grief was seated on some steps of rough-hewn stones. The glory of her hair swept about her knees. Her arms were empty; her hands locked; her head bent. Above stood a little child, with hand just extended to open a great door, which was about to open and admit him. He reached up his hand fearlessly ("and that is faith," thought Polly), and at the same time he glanced down at his weeping mother, as if to say, "Look up, mother dear! I am safely in."

Just then the choir burst into a grand hymn which was new to Polly, and which came to her with the force of a personal message:

"The Son of God goes forth to war,
A kingly crown to gain;
His blood-red banner streams afar—
Who follows in His train?
Who best can drink his cup of woe,
Triumphant over pain,
Who patient bears his cross below,
He follows in His train."

Verse after verse rang in splendid strength through the solemn aisles of the church, ending with the lines:

"O God, to us may strength be given
To follow in His train!"

Dr. George's voice came to Polly as it sounded that gray October afternoon beside the sea: "When the sun of one's happiness is set, one lights a candle called 'Patience,' and guides one's footsteps by that."

She leaned her head on the pew in front of her, and breathed a prayer. The minister was praying for the rest of the people, but she needed to utter her own thought just then.

"Father in heaven, I will try to follow; I have lighted my little candle, help me to keep it burning! I shall stumble often in the darkness, I know, for it was all so clear when I could walk by my darling mother's light, which was like the sun, so bright, so pure, so strong!

Help me to keep the little candle steady, so that it may throw its beams farther and farther into the pathway that now looks so dim."

Polly sank to sleep that night in her white bed in the Pilgrim Chamber; and the name of the chamber was Peace indeed, for she had a smile on her lips—a smile that looked as if the little candle had in truth been lighted in her soul, and was shining through her face as though it were a window.

XVII

Polly Launches Her Ships

THERE were great doings in the Birds' Nest.

A hundred dainty circulars, printed in black and scarlet on Irish linen paper, had been sent to those ladies on Mrs. Bird's calling list who had children between the ages of five and twelve, that being Polly's chosen limit of age.

These notes of invitation read as follows:

"Come, tell us a story!"

THE CHILDREN'S HOUR.

Mrs. Donald Bird requests the pleasure of your company from 4:30 to 5:30 o'clock on Mondays or Thursdays from November to March inclusive.

FIRST GROUP: Mondays. Children from 5 to 8 years.
SECOND GROUP: Thursdays.   "   "   8 " 12 years.

Each group limited in number to twenty-four.

Miss Pauline Oliver will tell stories suitable to
the ages of the children, adapted to their prevail-
ing interests, and appropriate to the special months
of the year.

These stories will be chosen with the greatest
care, and will embrace representative tales of all
classes—narrative, realistic, scientific, imaginative,
and historical. They will be illustrated by songs and
blackboard sketches. Terms for the Series (Twenty
Hours), Five Dollars.

R. S. V. P.

Polly felt an absolute sense of suffocation as she saw
Mrs. Bird seal and address the last square envelope.

"If anybody does come," she said somewhat sadly, "I
am afraid it will be only that the story hour is at your
lovely house."

"Don't be so foolishly independent, my child. If I
gather the groups, it is only you who will be able to
hold them together. I am your manager, and it is my
duty to make the accessories as perfect as possible.
When the scenery and costumes and stage settings are
complete, you enter and do the real work. I retire, and
the sole responsibility for success or failure rests upon
your shoulders; I should think that would be enough
to satisfy the most energetic young woman. I had decided on the library as the scene of action; an open
fire is indispensable, and that room is delightfully large
when the center table is lifted out: but I am afraid it is
hardly secluded enough, and that people might trouble

you by coming in; so what do you think of the music room upstairs? You will have your fire, your piano, plenty of space, and a private entrance for the chicks, who can lay their wraps in the hall as they pass up. I will take the large Turkish rug from the red guest chamber—that will make the room look warmer—and I have a dozen other charming devices."

"If I were half as sure of my part as I am of yours, dear Fairy Godmother, we should have nothing to fear. I have a general plan mapped out for the stories, but a great deal of the work will have to be done from week to week, as I go on. I shall use the same program in the main for both groups, but I shall simplify everything and illustrate more freely for the little ones, telling the historical and scientific stories with much more detail to the older group. This is what Mr. Bird calls my 'basic idea,' which will be filled out from week to week according to inspiration. For November, I shall make autumn, the harvest, and Thanksgiving the starting point. I am all ready with my historical story of 'The First Thanksgiving,' for I told it at the Children's Hospital last year, and it went beautifully.

"I have one doll dressed in Dutch costume, to show how the children looked that the little Pilgrims played with in Holland; and another dressed like a Puritan maiden, to show them the simple old New England gown. Then I have two fine pictures of Miles Standish and the Indian chief Massasoit.

"For December and January I shall have Christmas and winter, and frost and ice and snow, with the contrasts of eastern and Californian climates."

"I can get the Immigration Bureau to give you a percentage on that story, Polly," said Uncle Jack Bird, who had strolled in and taken a seat. "Just make your facts strong enough, and you can make a handsome thing out of that idea."

"Don't interrupt us, Jack," said Mrs. Bird, "and go directly out, if you please. You were not asked to this party."

"Where was I?" continued Polly. "Oh yes—the contrast between Californian and eastern winters; and January will have a moral story or two, you know—New Year's resolutions, and all that. February will be full of sentiment and patriotism—St. Valentine's Day and Washington's Birthday—I can hardly wait for that, there are so many lovely things to do in that month. March will bring in the first hint of spring. The winds will serve for my science story; and as it chances to be a presidential year, we will celebrate Inauguration Day, and have some history, if a good many subscribers come in."

"Why do you say 'if,' Polly? Multitudes of names are coming in. I have told you so from the beginning."

"Very well, then; when a sufficient number of names are entered, I should like to spend ten dollars on a very large sand-table, which I can use with the younger group for illustrations. It is perfectly clean work, and I have helped Miss Denison and her children to do the loveliest things with it. She makes geography lessons—plains, hills, mountains, valleys, rivers, and lakes; or the children make a picture of the story they have just heard. I saw them do 'Over the River and Through the

Wood to Grandfather's House We Go,' 'Washington's Winter Camp at Valley Forge,' and 'The Midnight Ride of Paul Revere.' I have ever so many songs chosen, and those for November and December are almost learned without my notes. I shall have to work very hard to be ready twice a week!"

"Too hard, I fear," said Mrs. Bird anxiously.

"Oh no; not a bit too hard! If the children are only interested, I shall not mind any amount of trouble. By the way, dear Mrs. Bird, you won't let the nurses or mothers stand in the doorways? You will please see that I am left quite alone with the children, won't you?"

"Certainly; no mothers shall be admitted, if they make you nervous; it is the children's hour. But after two or three months, when you have all become acquainted, and the children are accustomed to listening attentively, I almost hope you will allow a few nurses to come in and sit in the corners—the ones who bring the youngest children, for example; it would be such a means of education to them. There's another idea for you next year—a nurses' class in storytelling."

"It would be rather nice, wouldn't it?—and I should be older then, and more experienced. I really think I could do it, if Miss Denison would help me by talks and instructions. She will be here next year. Oh, how the little plan broadens out!"

"And, Polly, you have chosen to pay for your circulars, and propose to buy your sand-table. This I agree to, if you insist upon it; though why I shouldn't help my godchild I cannot quite understand. But knowing you were so absorbed in other matters that you

would forget the frivolities, and remembering that you
have been wearing the same two dresses for months, I
have ventured to get you some pretty gowns for the
'story hours,' and I want you to accept them for your
Christmas present. They will serve for all your 'afternoons' and for our home dinners, as you will not be
going out anywhere this winter."

"Oh, how kind you are, Mrs. Bird! You load me with
benefits, and how can I ever repay you?"

"You do not have to repay them to me necessarily,
my child; you can pass them over, as you will be constantly doing, to all these groups of children, day after
day. I am a sort of stupid, rich old lady who serves as
a source of supply. My chief brilliancy lies in devising
original methods of getting rid of my surplus in all sorts
of odd and delightful ways, left untried, for the most
part, by other people. I've been buying up splendid old
trees in the outskirts of certain New England country
towns—trees that were in danger of being cut down for
wood. Twenty-five to forty dollars buys a glorious tree,
and it is safe for ever and ever to give shade to the tired
traveler and beauty to the landscape. Each of my boys
has his pet odd scheme for helping the world to 'go
right.' Donald, for instance, puts stamps on the unstamped letters displayed in the Cambridge post office,
and sends them spinning on their way. He never re-
ceives the thanks of the careless writers, but he takes
pleasure in making things straight. Paul writes me from
Phillips Academy that this year he is sending the nine
Ruggles children (a poor family of our acquaintance)
to some sort of entertainment once every month. Hugh
has just met a lovely girl who has induced him to help

Nobody could decide which was the loveliest dress

her maintain a boarding establishment for sick and deserted cats and dogs; and there we are!"

"But I'm a young, strong girl, and I fear I'm not so worthy an object of charity as a tree, an unstamped letter, an infant Ruggles, or a deserted cat! Still, I know the dresses will be lovely, and I had quite forgotten that I must be clothed in purple and fine linen for five months to come. It would have been one of my first thoughts last year, I am afraid; but lately this black dress has shut everything else from my sight."

"It was my thought that you should give up your black dress just for these occasions, dear, and wear something more cheerful for the children's sake. The dresses are very simple, for I've heard you say you can never tell a story when you are 'dressed up,' but they will please you, I know. They will be brought home this evening, and you must slip them all on, and show yourself to us in each."

They would have pleased anybody, even a princess, Polly thought, as she stood before her bed that evening patting the four pretty new dresses, and smoothing with childlike delight the folds of the four pretty skirts. It was such an odd sensation to have four dresses at a time!

They were of simple and inexpensive materials, as was appropriate; but Mrs. Bird's exquisite taste and feeling for what would suit Polly's personality made them more attractive than if they had been rich or expensive.

There was a white China silk, with belt and shoulder knots of black velvet; a white Japanese crepe, with

purple lilacs strewed over its surface, and frills of violet
ribbon for ornament; a Christmas dress of soft white
camel's hair, with bands of white-fox fur round the
slightly pointed neck and elbow-sleeves; and, last of all,
a Quaker gown of silver-gray nun's cloth, with a surplice and full undersleeves of white crepe.

"I'm going to be vain, Mrs. Bird!" cried Polly, with
compunction in her voice. "I've never had a real beautiful, undyed, un-made-over dress in my whole life, and
I shall never have strength of character to own four at
once without being vain!"

This speech was uttered through the crack of the
library door, outside of which Polly stood, gathering
courage to walk in and be criticised.

"Think of your aspiring nose, Sapphira!" came from
a voice within.

"Oh, are you there too, Edgar?"

"Of course I am, and so is Tom Mills. The news that
you are going to 'try on' is all over the neighborhood!
If you have cruelly fixed the age limit so that we can't
possibly get in to the performances, we are going to
attend all the dress rehearsals. Oh, ye little fishes! What
a seraphic Sapphira! I wish Tony were here!"

She was pretty, there was no doubt about it, as she
turned around like a revolving wax figure in a show
window, and assumed absurd fashion-plate attitudes;
and pretty chiefly because of the sparkle, intelligence,
sunny temper, and vitality that made her so magnetic.

Nobody could decide which was the loveliest dress,
even when she had appeared in each one twice. In the
lilac and white crepe, with a bunch of dark Parma

violets thrust in her corsage, Uncle Jack called her a poem. Edgar asserted openly that in the Christmas dress he should like to have her modeled in wax and put in a glass case on his table; but Mrs. Bird and Tom Mills voted for the Quaker gray, in which she made herself inexpressibly demure by braiding her hair in two discreet braids down her back.

"The dress rehearsal is over. Good night all!" she said, as she took her candle. "I will say 'handsome is as handsome does' fifty times before I go to sleep, and perhaps—I only say perhaps—I may be used to my beautiful clothes in a week or two, so that I shall be my usual modest self again."

"Good-night, Polly," said the boys, "we will see you tomorrow."

" 'Pauline,' if you please, not 'Polly.' I ceased to be Polly this morning when the circulars were posted. I am now Miss Pauline Oliver, storyteller by profession."